to Bobbie from Ma

ZAUBERLINDA
The Wise Witch

By
EVA
KATHARINE
GIBSON

Robt. Smith
Printing Co.
Publishers
CHICAGO. LANSING.

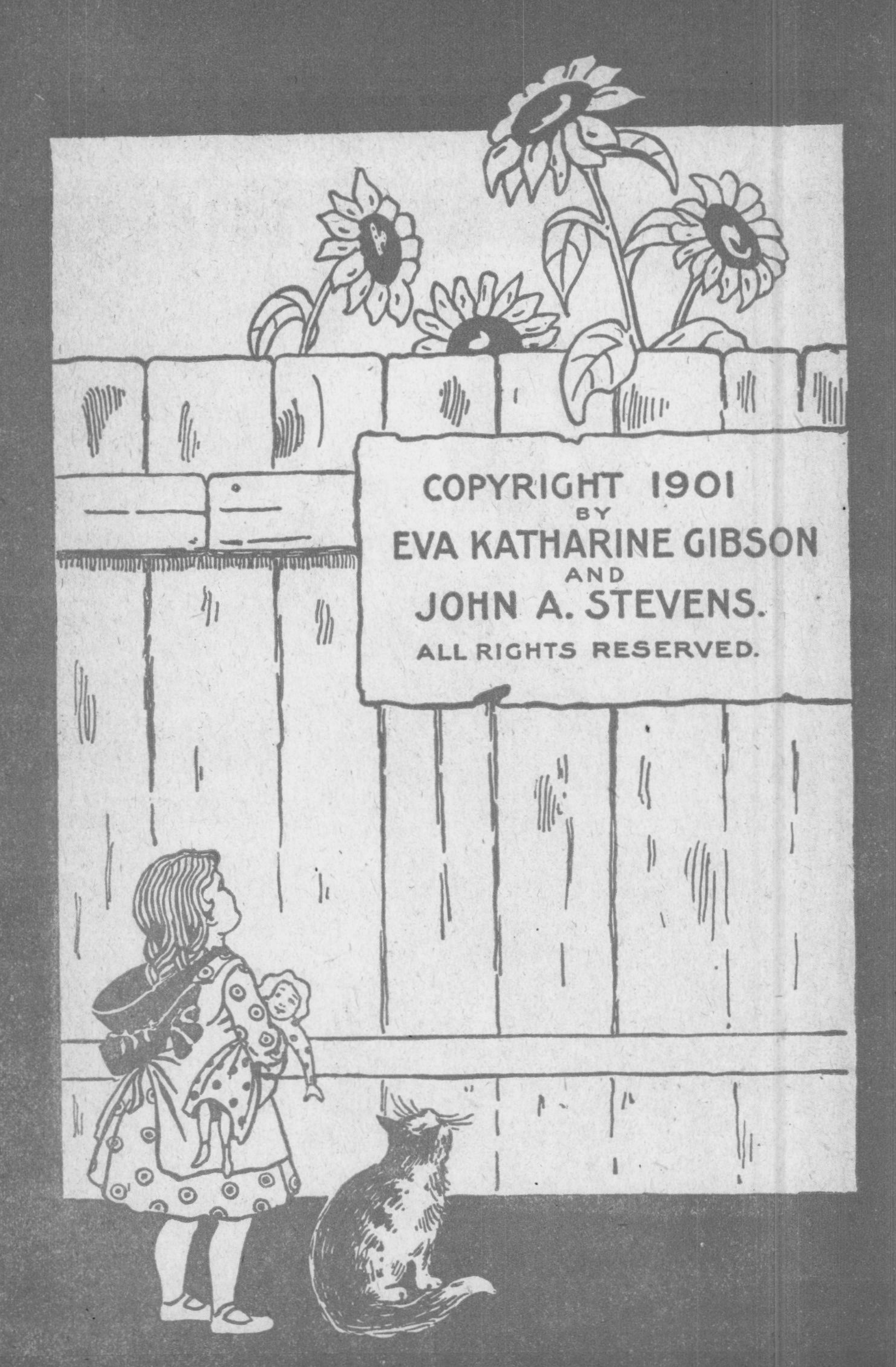
COPYRIGHT 1901
BY
EVA KATHARINE GIBSON
AND
JOHN A. STEVENS.
ALL RIGHTS RESERVED.

To
Dear Little Helen Stevens
This Book
is
Affectionately Inscribed
by
Her Friend

THE AUTHOR

Pictures
by
Mabel Tibbitts.

LIST OF CHAPTERS

INTRODUCTION

This Fairy Tale, the scenes of which are laid in the Northwest, is an attempt to unite the rich Legend of Older Lands with the Fact and Fancy of the New World. An opportunity for this has been offered by the Mystery and Romance associated with the Black Hills in the imagination of the Dakota Indians.

It is hoped that the story may stimulate an interest in the Wonders of Nature, and engender love and sympathy for those of Her creatures who cannot speak for themselves.

If the reader finds in this narrative of Annie's Wanderings, the pleasure found by the author in recording them, the story will have fulfilled its purpose.

We believe the book may safely be placed in the hands of all children between the years of seven and ninety-seven.

Chapter I
Annie's Home

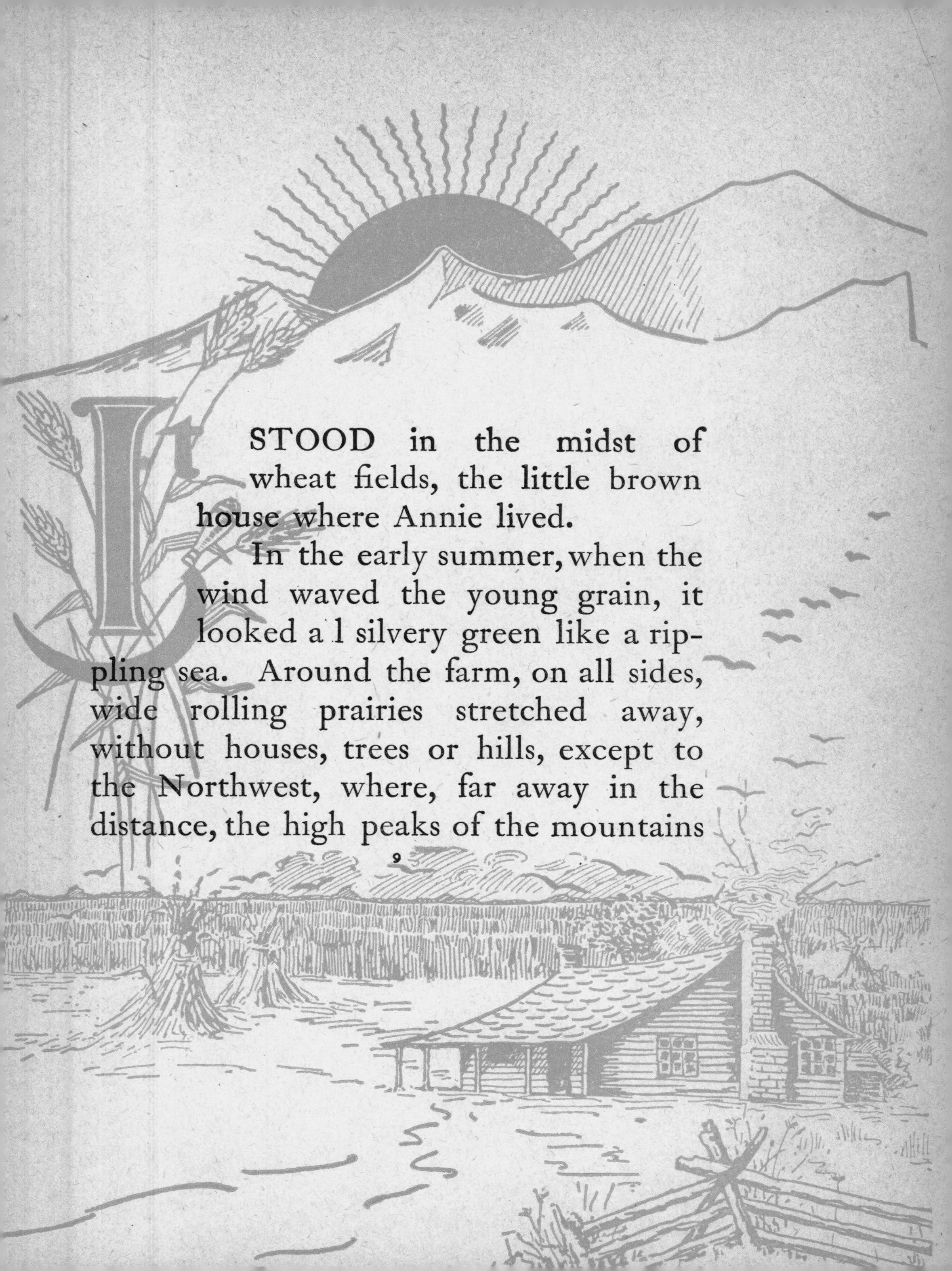

It STOOD in the midst of wheat fields, the little brown house where Annie lived.

In the early summer, when the wind waved the young grain, it looked a l silvery green like a rippling sea. Around the farm, on all sides, wide rolling prairies stretched away, without houses, trees or hills, except to the Northwest, where, far away in the distance, the high peaks of the mountains known as the Black Hills, stood up clear and dark against the deep blue Dakota sky.

Annie, who was a thoughtful little girl, would often pause in her work or play, and stand watching those distant hills that seemed to rise abruptly from the level plains.

The prairies around her were, in many ways, beautiful, but they were not forever changing in appearance, as were the hills.

When the sun was shining the peaks stood out very clearly, purple and dark. When it rained, they looked shadowy and cloud-like.

After a sultry, hot day the black thunder clouds would roll up in the

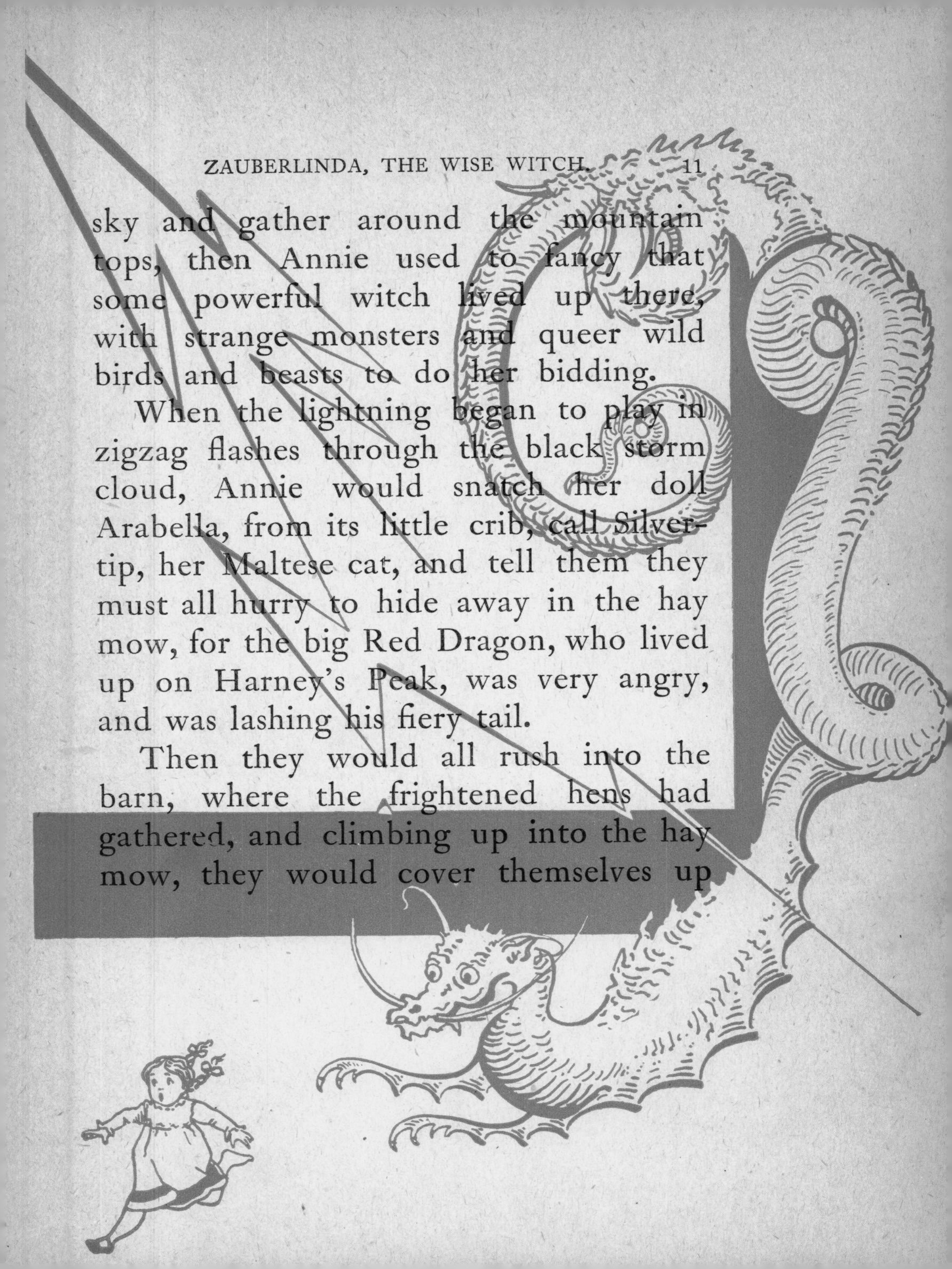

sky and gather around the mountain tops, then Annie used to fancy that some powerful witch lived up there, with strange monsters and queer wild birds and beasts to do her bidding.

When the lightning began to play in zigzag flashes through the black storm cloud, Annie would snatch her doll Arabella, from its little crib, call Silvertip, her Maltese cat, and tell them they must all hurry to hide away in the hay mow, for the big Red Dragon, who lived up on Harney's Peak, was very angry, and was lashing his fiery tail.

Then they would all rush into the barn, where the frightened hens had gathered, and climbing up into the hay mow, they would cover themselves up with the fragrant dry grass, and wait until the thunder-shower was over.

Annie had to make up plays and games for herself, for their nearest neighbor, Nils Nilson, a Norwegian farmer, lived eight miles away, and as the little girl had no brothers or sisters, her only playmates were Arabella and her Maltese cat, who was called Silvertip, because he was all a beautiful dark blue color, except the tip of his tail, which was pure white.

Annie had brought him up by hand, for he had been given to her when he was only a little, weak, helpless kitten; she had taken such good care of him, that now, although a young cat, he was very big and strong and so knowing that he understood nearly everything his little mistress said to him.

He used to tell Annie about his adventures, in his queer cat way, and would become very much excited if she did not seem to understand all he said.

He followed her everywhere. When she watered her flowers, or went to the barn to hunt for eggs, or down to the creek to gather cowslips. In fact, Silvertip was such a wise and brave and cunning cat, that he was a splendid companion, and Annie thought the world of him. Yet, good as he was, he was still not quite without faults.

He was rough and boisterous in his play at times, being a boy cat, and he

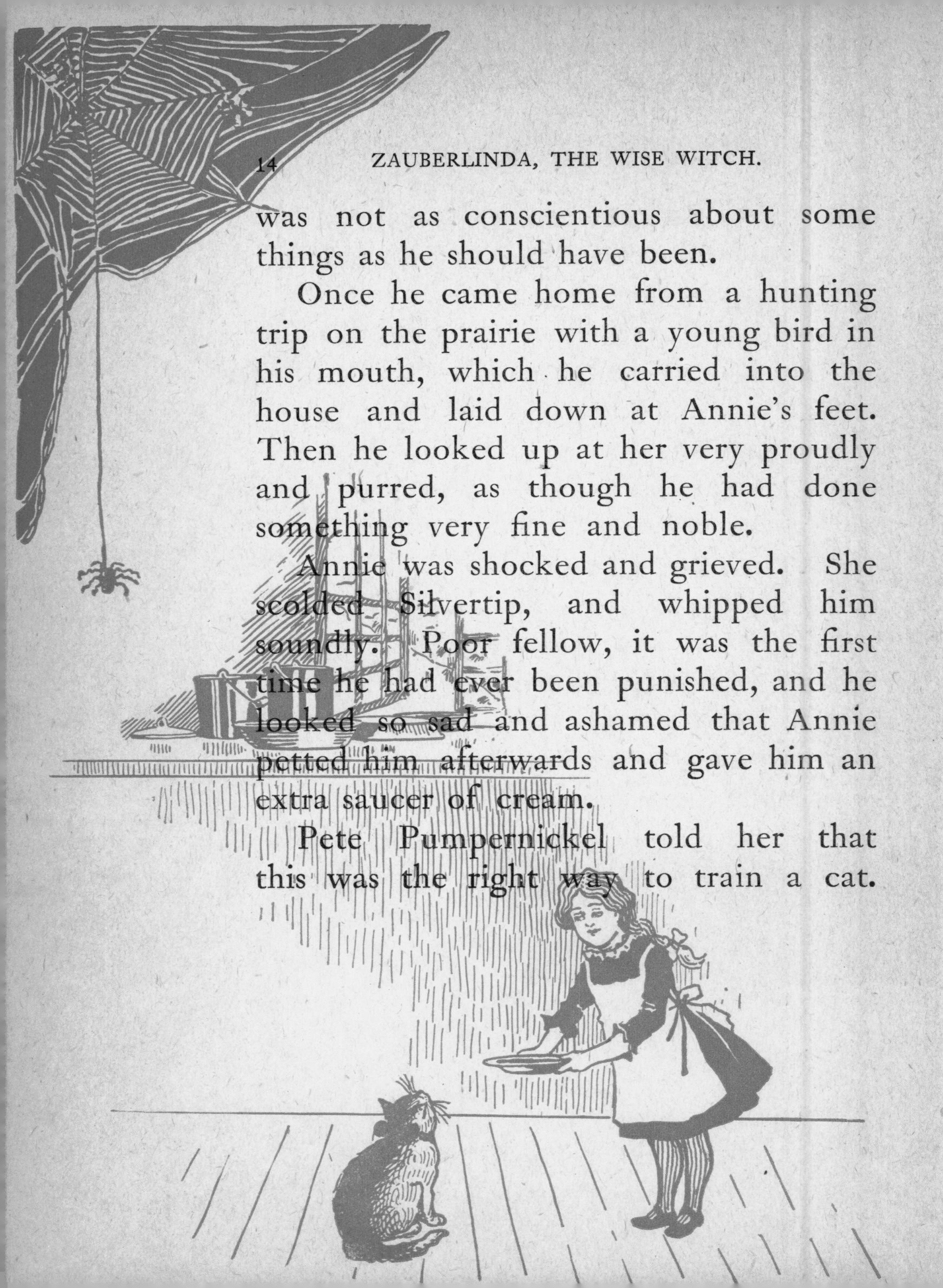

was not as conscientious about some things as he should have been.

Once he came home from a hunting trip on the prairie with a young bird in his mouth, which he carried into the house and laid down at Annie's feet. Then he looked up at her very proudly and purred, as though he had done something very fine and noble.

Annie was shocked and grieved. She scolded Silvertip, and whipped him soundly. Poor fellow, it was the first time he had ever been punished, and he looked so sad and ashamed that Annie petted him afterwards and gave him an extra saucer of cream.

Pete Pumpernickel told her that this was the right way to train a cat.

After that Silvertip let the innocent birds alone and only caught rats and mice.

Annie's mother had died when she was a baby, and so her father had brought her out to South Dakota to live with her grandmother on the farm.

Her father was away from home most of the time. He was "prospecting" up among the hills, which means that he was looking for a gold mine.

Annie was very anxious to have him find it, for when he should be lucky enough to find a mine it would make them all rich, and then Annie's father had promised to move to town and send his little daughter to school.

It seemed to her as though they had been waiting and hoping and waiting to find this gold mine ever since she could remember. Sometimes she grew almost discouraged, but Mr. McLane was a cheerful man, and was sure that they would "strike it rich," as he called it, very, very soon.

Annie's grandmother was a good, kind woman, and a nice housekeeper. She could make such delicious strawberry shortcake that there never was any left, when they had company.

The little girl's grandmother loved her dearly, but there was always so much work to be done, that she never found time to talk with the child, when Annie wanted to know why everything was so strange and beautiful in the world around her. Why the

colors on the butterfly's wings were so gay? Why the wild geese always flew in such a queer shaped flock? Why the dragon fly had such bright eyes? What the katydids were always talking about? How the swallows happened to know just the right time to fly northward, and a great many other things,—then her grandmother would say, "There, there, child, you will drive me wild with your foolish questions, run away and play, I'm too busy to bother with you now."

This hurt Annie's feelings, for she felt so little, and the world seemed so strange and big, and there were so many things to learn, and no way of finding out about them unless some one would take time to answer her questions.

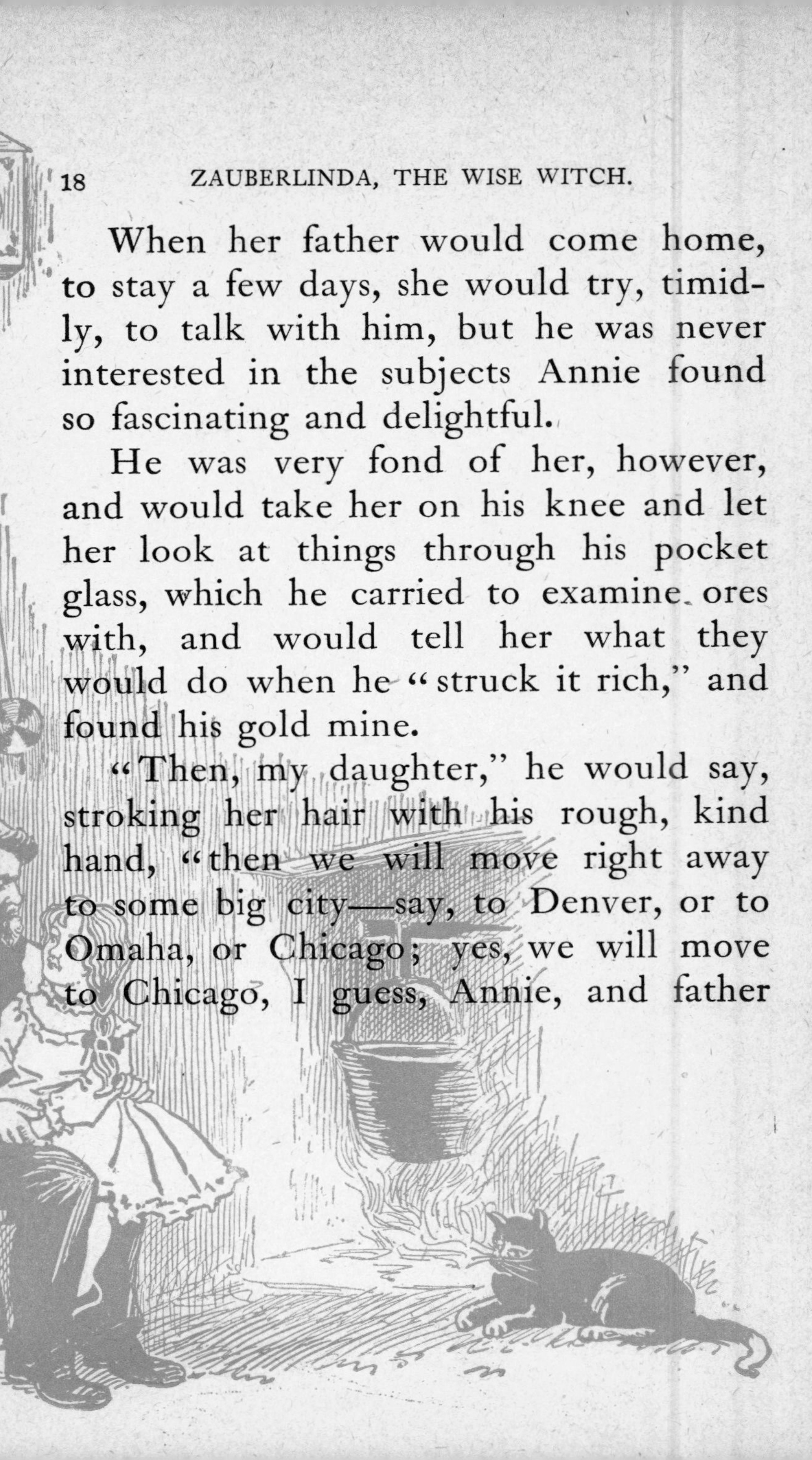

When her father would come home, to stay a few days, she would try, timidly, to talk with him, but he was never interested in the subjects Annie found so fascinating and delightful.

He was very fond of her, however, and would take her on his knee and let her look at things through his pocket glass, which he carried to examine ores with, and would tell her what they would do when he "struck it rich," and found his gold mine.

"Then, my daughter," he would say, stroking her hair with his rough, kind hand, "then we will move right away to some big city—say, to Denver, or to Omaha, or Chicago; yes, we will move to Chicago, I guess, Annie, and father will hire a lady to teach you everything. She shall have nothing else to do all day long but to answer your questions and teach you to play on the piano." Usually, after saying this, her father would take a bit of ore out of his pocket and look at it carefully through his pocket glass, turning it over, and examining it upon every side very thoroughly.

Then he and his hired man, Pete Pumpernickel, would sit, talking of ores and mines, while the sun sank down in the western plains and the fire-flies began their dance over the wheat fields, while the bats came out and circled about their heads and Annie would leave them to go in and put Arabella to bed.

Chapter II
Annie's Friends and Pets

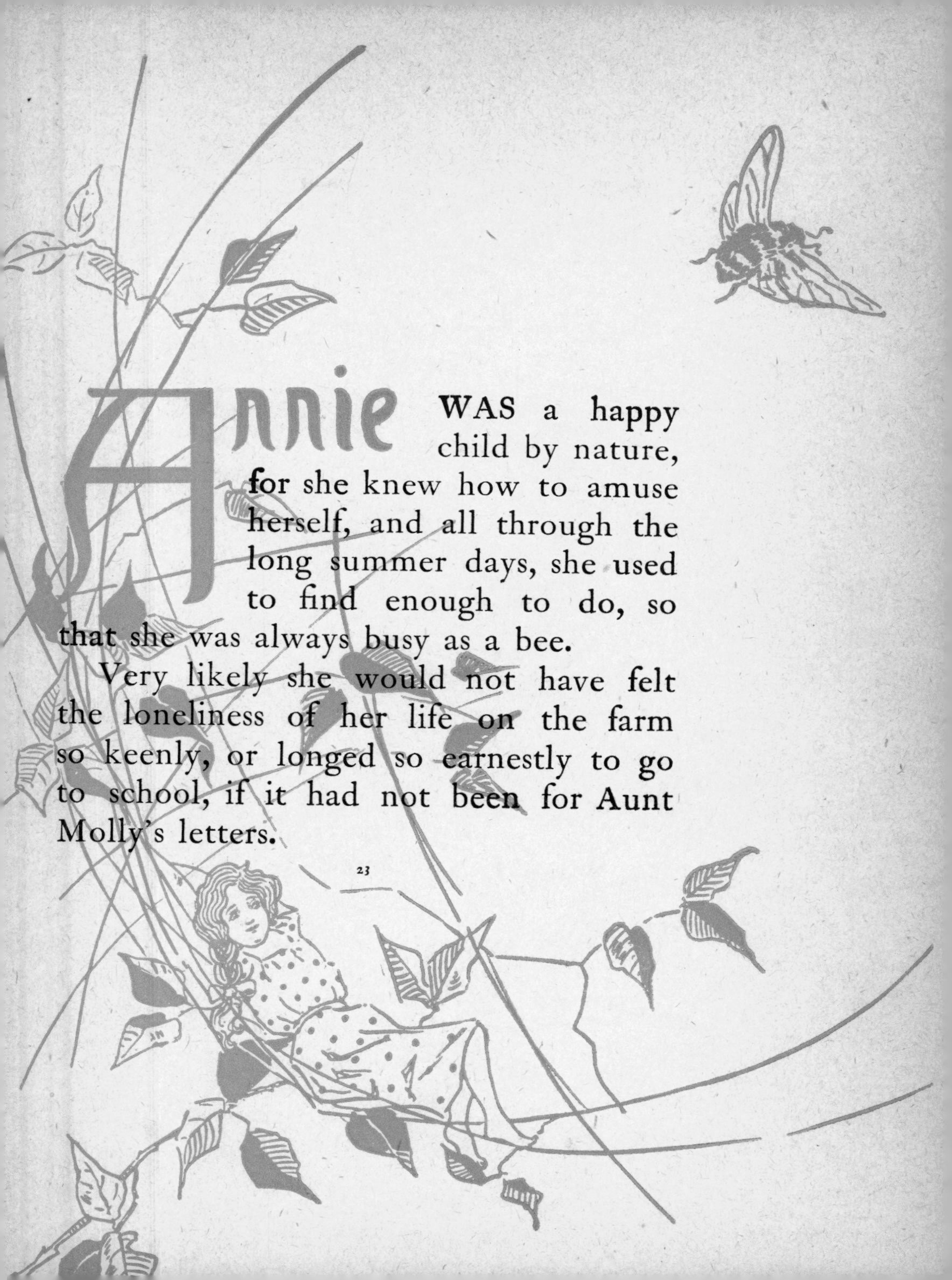

ANNIE WAS a happy child by nature, for she knew how to amuse herself, and all through the long summer days, she used to find enough to do, so that she was always busy as a bee.

Very likely she would not have felt the loneliness of her life on the farm so keenly, or longed so earnestly to go to school, if it had not been for Aunt Molly's letters.

Aunt Molly was the sister of Annie's dead mother. She lived in Chicago, and used to write often to Annie's grandmother, inquiring about her small niece.

The grandmother would read these letters to Annie. Somehow, after one of Aunt Molly's letters, the little girl used always to feel herself very ignorant, but as she was a sensitive child with a great deal of pride in her character, she would not have told this feeling of hers to any one but Silvertip or Arabella for the world.

Aunt Molly used to write of what Lizzie May, Annie's six-year-old cousin, was learning at kindergarten and how she hoped that Annie, her dear sister's child, might come East some day and go to school, and not be allowed to run wild on the Dakota prairie until she grew up into a perfect savage.

Nearly always after reading one of these letters, Annie's grandmother would push her spectacles back upon her forehead, smooth down her apron and, looking very solemn, call the little girl to her. Annie would lean against her knee and look up earnestly into the wrinkled, kind face.

The grandmother would say, "Annie, it is high time you were learning something. Now tell me, child, how much six times four is." Annie would blush red under her freckles, for she well knew that she was weak in the sixes, but at

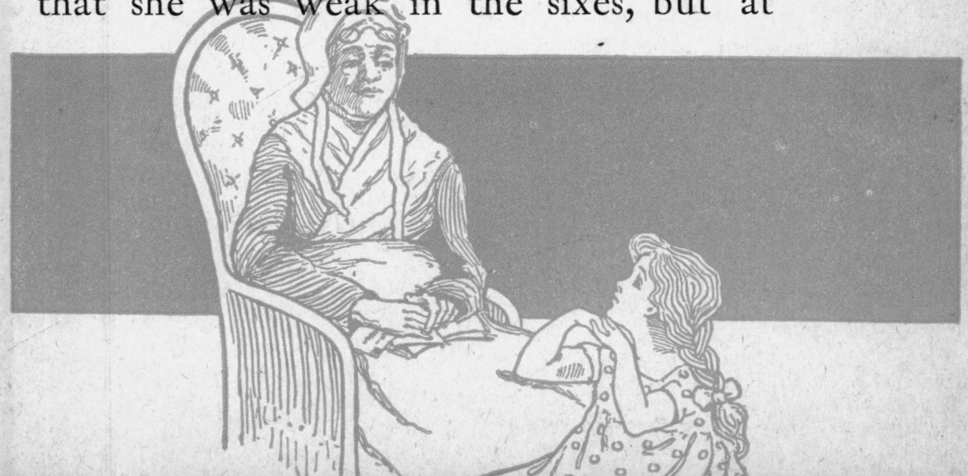

last she would stammer, "six times four is forty-eight." Then if her father was sitting by, he would laugh at her and grandmother would say, "Oh, Annie, can't you answer such a simple question as that?" And Annie, in her mind, would repeat over nearly all the numbers in that old multiplication table, but somehow always seem to hit upon just the wrong answer as to how much six times four is, though her father would always try to signal the right answer to her behind grandmother's back.

Then grandmother would sigh, shake her head sadly and say, "Its no use, John, that child'll never know anything until she is sent to school regularly. Molly's girl, Lizzie May, is a year younger than our Annie, and she can say the multiplication tables right through, without stopping, clear up to the sevens."

Annie would step softly out of the room, feeling very crushed and foolish, and just of no earthly account in this world.

She was not a vain child at any time, and these sudden examinations in arithmetic took away from her just the very last little bit of faith and pride in herself that she had ever possessed.

She dreaded the coming of these letters, and bitterly regretted her ignorance. She began to think of the time when her father might find the gold mine, and to wonder if there was no way in which she could help him to luck, so that she

might go to school and learn things, like Lizzie May, in Chicago.

Yet Annie was not entirely alone. While she had no children for companions, she had many little playmates who, while dumb so far as our way of talking goes, still knew how to show their love for Annie, and their delight in her companionship, and it was a great comfort to her to feel that these friends were always loyal and liked her just as she was, and did not lose respect for her, even though she could never tell how much was six times four.

Besides Billy, the burro, and the new calf, there was a whole collection of pets, which she was always adding to by bringing in some little lost or injured stranger from the swamp or prairie, to be fed and cared for.

Then there were three beautiful little bantam chickens, that had been given to her. She had named the small white hen Snowflake. One of the bantam roosters she called Pantallettes, because the feathers grew down around his legs just like little white ruffles.

The other one was a proud, fierce, tiny fellow, who had Spanish blood in his veins. He was black as a coal. Annie called this one Captain Gib, after a friend of her father's.

I am sorry to relate that Captain Gib turned out to be a terrible fighter. Poor Pantallettes often had to be protected from him.

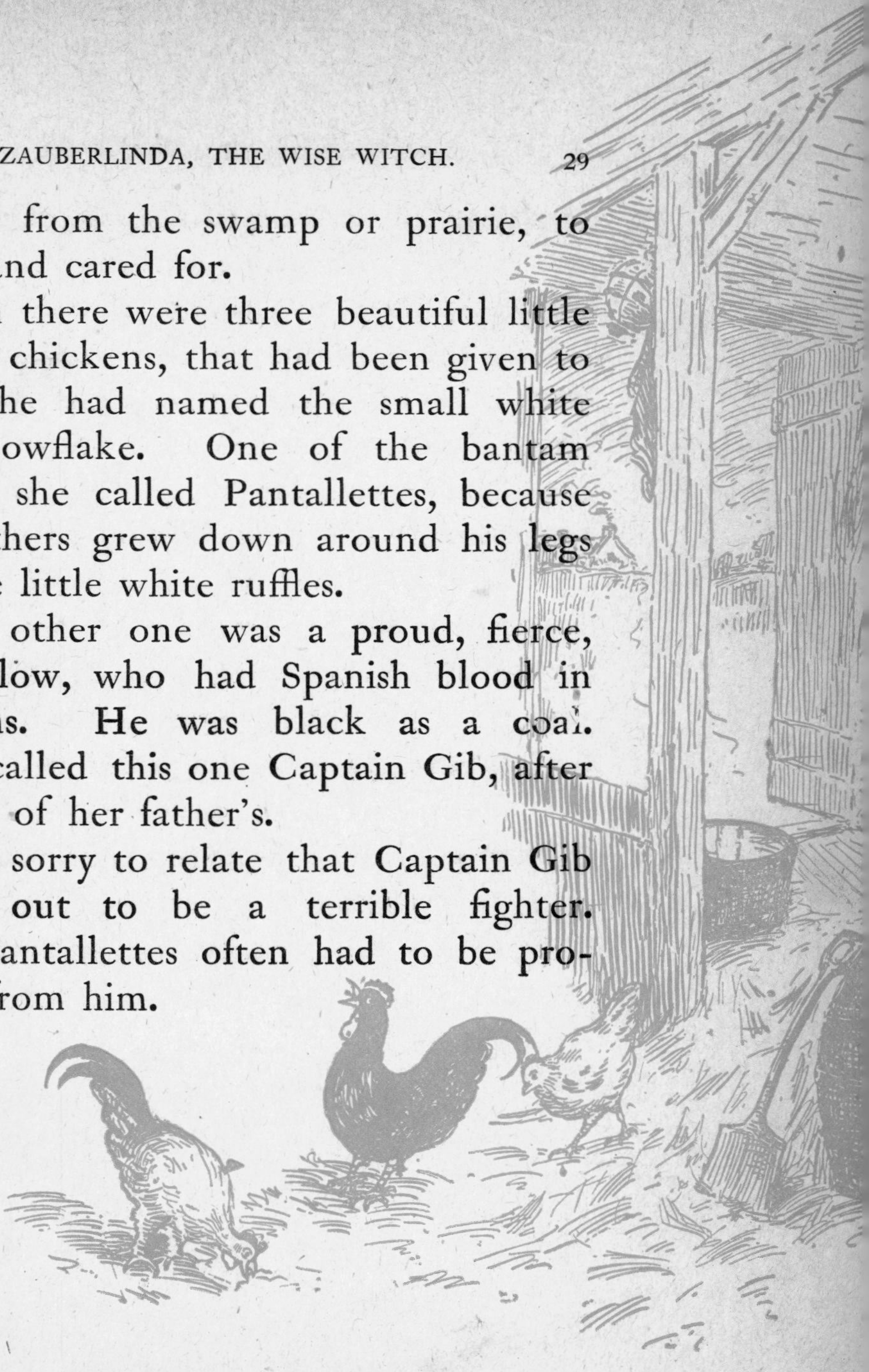

Then there were two young prairie hens, in modest brown dresses. On one of her long walks over the prairie, Annie had picked them up when they were but soft balls of yellow down. A cruel hunter had shot their mother and left them orphaned. Annie took them home and brought them up with the bantams.

The whole flock would come running and flying when she called them, and would light on her shoulders, or gather about her feet clucking and chirping from pure joy.

She seemed to have the knack of curing the hurts of the birds and other little wild creatures.

She had a pet gopher, that she picked up one day in the fields, with a broken leg; Pete Pumpernickel helped her make some splints to brace the leg up, and the gopher got well and could run about as briskly as ever; but it would not leave the farm house where it had been so kindly treated, and stayed on with them, as tame as the bantams.

Of all Annie's little dumb friends, only one had ever been so ungrateful as to run away after she had cured it. This affair had happened upon her birthday, when she was just six, one year before the wonderful trip into Pix-Sylvania, the land of Elves, the story of which is told in the second and third parts of this book.

Chapter III

The Rescue of the Young Prairie Dog

IT WAS in June, and the longest day of the year. Annie was out on the prairie looking for wild strawberries, for it was about the time they ripen in South Dakota.

Suddenly, as she stooped to pick a cluster of big berries, she was startled by hearing a pitiful little squeak, and looking down at her feet she saw a rabbit trap, partly hidden by grass and flowers, with a young prairie dog caught in it by the paw.

As the little creature looked up at her with its wild, bright eyes, the expression of fear and pain in them went straight to the girl's kind heart. "Oh, you poor little thing, I will set you free," she cried. She had often seen the trappers go by her home with traps like this, and Pete had shown her how to set and open one.

She went to work very carefully to pry open its ugly jaws, with their cruel, sharp teeth. Now, when the little captive realized that it was not to be harmed, but was to be set free, it looked up at her again, and Annie never forgot that look of gratitude.

It tried to limp away, but could not; its paw had been too badly crushed in the trap. Very tenderly Annie took it in her arms and carried it home. She made it a bed of nice clean straw and gave it water. It drank a little, but refused to eat anything, and sat very still, as though thinking earnestly. Now happened something that was exceedingly strange. Annie's other wild pets, the gopher and the prairie hens, would not even stay to look upon the stranger, but appeared so afraid, that Annie was surprised.

In fact, all of the animals avoided this queer little creature. Sometimes Spot, the old cow, and her red calf and Billy, the burro, and old "Yeller," the dog, and Silvertip, would form in a wide circle around the crippled prairie dog and stand looking at it in a wild, frightened way, with their eyes bulging out.

Finally old Spot would shake her horns and bellow, and turn and run as though half crazy, while the others would follow her at full speed.

It was certainly strange, yet it made Annie indignant to see them so silly, and afraid of a little prairie dog with a crushed paw.

When Pete came home from the hay field that night, she told him about it. To her surprise, Pete, instead of laughing, looked quite solemn, and throwing down his hay fork, went at once to look at her new pet.

He was a long time examining the strange little creature, and was careful not to touch it. At last he shook his head and said, "It is unheimlich, mein Annie." "Unheimlich," inquired the child, "what does that mean, Pete?" "I cannot just tell it in the English words, but it means that this little animal is not a common prairie dog. He is not really a prairie dog at all, but one of the 'little folks' in the skin of a prairie dog," said Pete. "What day of the month is this, mein Annie?" "Why, it is the 21st of June, my birthday," said Annie.

"Potstausend, then it is surely one of the 'Little Hill Men' disguised in this way, for on Midsummer day—just that one day in all the year—the Great Wise Witch, Zauberlinda, lets the little hill folks come up from their own country, deep down in the earth, and wander around for a little time.

"Oh, it is great luck, if you do one of them a kindness then, for they will never forget it; but bad luck will follow all the year if you should hurt one.

"Now, perhaps the King of the 'Little Hill Folks' will show your father where the rich gold ore is, and so make us all rich." Just then Marthy Stubbs came out of the back door with a bowl of Indian meal dough for the turkeys.

"Ach, ya," Pete went on, "mein Annie, they are very wonderful these gnomes, we Hartz people call them the 'Hill Folks.' They make beautiful cups of gold and silver, and—" "Did you ever see one yourself?" asked Marthy

scornfully, as she threw out her last handful of corn meal.

"Oh, no, I have not just with mein own eyes seen a little 'Hill Man,' but many of my friends, back there in the Hartz country of my Fatherland have," said Pete, with an injured look, lighting his big pipe and pulling his hat down lower over his eyes.

"Humph! if you Germans ain't the craziest lot I ever *did* see," said Marthy Stubbs, but Marthy never believed anything, so her opinion did not have much influence upon Annie's faith in Pete, for, while it may be foolish to believe quite everything that is told one, it is certainly just as senseless to close one's heart and mind against everything beautiful and strange, by stupidly refusing to believe in anything outside of one's own narrow experience.

Whether Annie's new pet was really a Gnome in disguise, or just a prairie dog, it acted very strangely. That queer, wild look in its eyes still seemed to frighten away the other animals. Even Captain Gib, who was, by nature, as brave as a lion, and who lorded it over roosters five times his own size—even *he* gave that prairie dog a wide berth. Annie was its only protector and friend. It seemed quite fond of her, and would eat out of her hand, but would not allow anyone else to touch it.

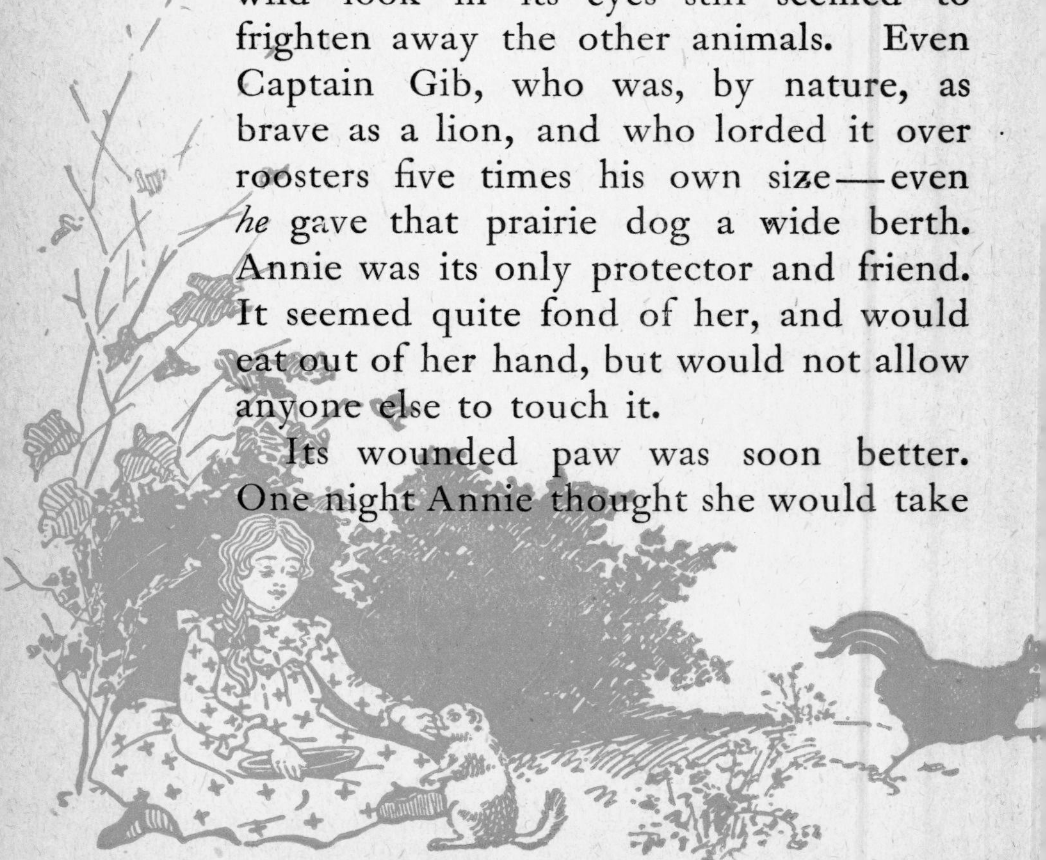

Its wounded paw was soon better. One night Annie thought she would take it out of her room and put it in the cunning little house that Pete had built for it out of an old wooden box. This little house had a small door cut in one end, with a little padlock on the outside. Annie put the prairie dog in its new home, gave it food and water, locked the door and went to bed.

The next morning when she went out to see how he liked his new quarters, she unlocked the door and called, just as she had always done when she fed him, but he did not come at her call. Everything was silent, empty and deserted; not even one hair was there left of him. His prairie dogship had vanished, and no one could tell how he had got away, where he had gone to, or why he had left them, after receiving at their hands such kind treatment.

Who had let him out? Not a hole could be found anywhere around through which he could have burrowed his way to liberty, and Annie had the key to the door of his little house with her.

It certainly was a very great mystery. Then Pete said that if he was a Gnome in disguise, it would have been easy for him to pick any kind of a lock, as all Gnomes are expert metal workers. Even Marthy Stubbs, for once, did not laugh at this, for how else could so strange a disappearance be accounted for?

This affair had happened when Annie was six years old—one year before the time when she took her strange journey

into the country of the Gnomes, and that queer kingdom of the Elves, which is called Pix-Sylvania, in the midst of which lies the beautiful Enchanted Wood.

The little girl grieved over her odd pet's unkind behavior, for she had really done everything in her power to make that prairie dog happy, and then for him to run away without one good-bye look at her was really too bad.

It was her first experience of ingratitude, and gave her a poor opinion of prairie dogs, although before this they had always interested her, for they seemed such cunning, intelligent little animals, living almost like human beings, in regular towns or communities on the prairies, where the traveller may see hundreds of the small mounds which mark their underground homes, all grouped together. Here, too, in the cold winter time, lives the small grey prairie owl, who creeps into the warm houses of the prairie dogs and lives with them in peace and harmony.

They are certainly very intelligent creatures, but, thought Annie, what is intelligence alone, without love and gratitude? But we must always be slow to distrust our friends—even when appearances are against them, and this is a truth that Annie was to learn later on; for at heart there are really very few creatures, either human beings or animals, or dwellers in Fairyland, who are really ungrateful, for the greatest power on earth is the power of kindness. Everything that lives—the flowers, trees, birds, bees, animals, and men and women—are influenced and changed by it.

If you do not believe this, take something, or someone, and try it upon them for a time, and you will soon come to acknowledge its truth.

One thing was deeply impressed upon Annie's mind after this episode of the prairie dog. Pete Pumpernickel was a wonderful fellow and knew a great deal. She made up her mind to learn all she could from him about these Gnomes and Elves and Pixies, for who knows when or where such knowledge might not prove most useful?

Chapter IV

Pete Pumpernickel tells about the Fairies

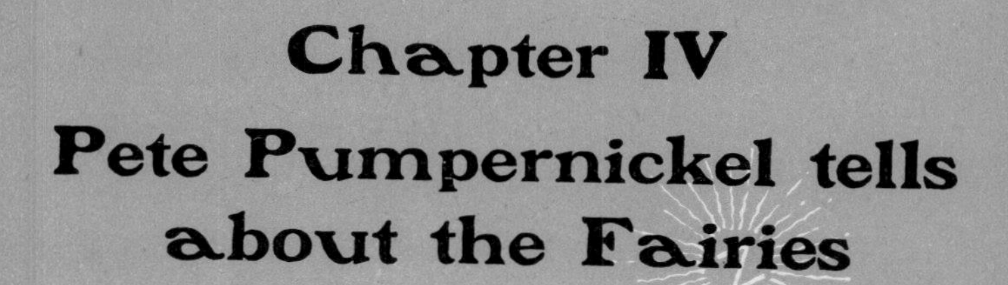

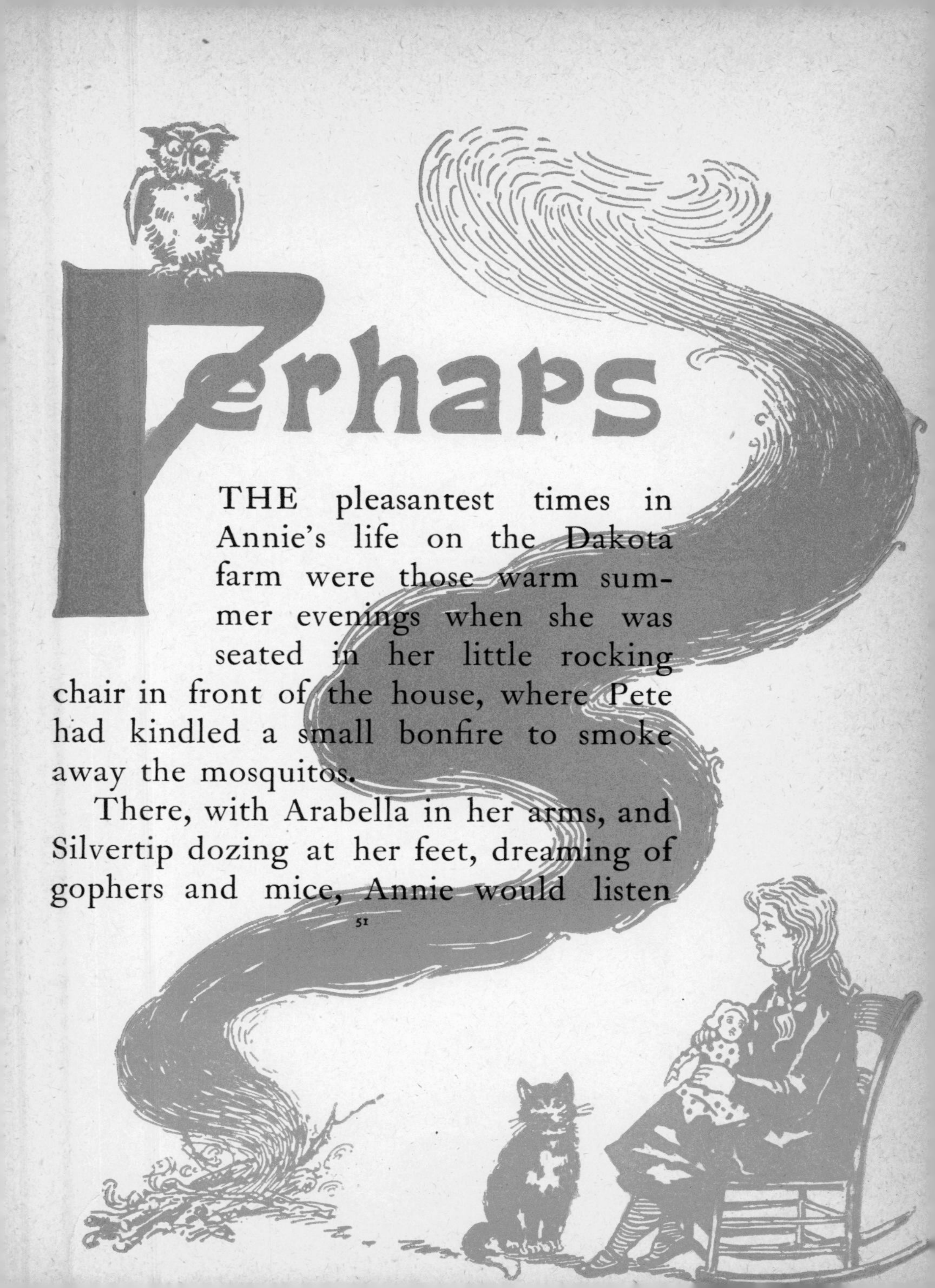

Perhaps

THE pleasantest times in Annie's life on the Dakota farm were those warm summer evenings when she was seated in her little rocking chair in front of the house, where Pete had kindled a small bonfire to smoke away the mosquitos.

There, with Arabella in her arms, and Silvertip dozing at her feet, dreaming of gophers and mice, Annie would listen while Pete played beautiful tunes on his harmonica, or told her wonderful stories of the Hartz Mountains, and the queer Witches, Elves and Gnomes, who are said to make their homes in the vales and caverns of the lonely hills. These evenings were the bright spots in the life of the lonesome child.

Here was the place where they all rested and talked together after the long day's work was over, after the cows were milked and the chickens had gone to roost, and when everything looked peaceful and beautiful in the moonlight.

Here her grandmother would come, still busy knitting the stockings for winter, or perhaps stirring the batter for the next morning's pancakes, yet really

quite as interested in Pete's stories as Annie herself.

Annie's father, too, would join them when he happened to be at home, and would tell stories of his adventures "prospecting" in the Black Hills.

Professor Phineas Pratt — a very learned man, who stopped with them when he came out from Massachusetts, hunting for fossils in the Bad Lands — would tell them about the enormous animals which had lived thousands of years before, the Glyptodon, the Pterodactyl, and others, whose entire race had vanished from the earth now, as had the giant ferns and the strange flowers and plants. The skeletons of those long-dead animals were often found in these parts, and were eagerly collected for museums of science and learning.

Upon these moonlit summer evenings, when Pete played one of his odd, wild tunes, old Jeff and Jerry, the big farm horses, would saunter along up from their pasture, and, coming as near as they possibly could to the musician, would lean their heads over the barnyard gate, point their ears forward and would stare with all their big, intelligent eyes, listening as though charmed by Pete's music. Presently Billy, the shaggy little Burro, would follow them, and after listening a moment would lift up his own shrill voice, joining in with his "he-haw, he-haw, he-haw," as if to say, "I like that; go on, go on."

It was pleasant for Annie to sit there and dream, even when awake, as she watched the distant mountain peaks, while around her the June bugs bumped and boomed along the dusk, and Silver-tip, waking from his doze, would leap up and try to catch them.

When Pete played a certain lively tune, old Spot, the brindle cow, would come up from her evening meal of sweet, green grass, with her awkward little calf frisking and leaping behind her. She would shake her horns and bellow, and prance so awkwardly about, excited by the music, that it would set the folks all laughing. Then Pete would take his harmonica down from his mouth and say softly: — "Potstauzend! A cow which

loves music as much as that must have been born in Germany."

Pete, himself, was born in Germany, in a little village near Ilsenburg, in the Hartz Mountains, close by the old city of Goslar. His parents were very poor, so Pete, when he was nineteen, had taken his few clothes, his pipe and his harmonica, made them up into a tidy bundle wrapped safely in a gay cotton handkerchief, and bidding parents and friends an affectionate farewell, had started for America to seek his fortune. After landing in New York he had come straight out to Dakota, where Mr. McLane, Annie's father, had hired him. He had been with the family now for a little over two years.

Pete was good natured, and Annie used to think him very nice looking when dressed in his best suit. On week days he went around in a checked gingham shirt, blue overalls and an old torn straw hat; but on Sundays he used to wear a suit made of bright blue woolen cloth. The coat was very long in the waist, and was trimmed with brass buttons. Pete added to this the big silver watch which had come down to him from his great grandfather; then, as a finishing touch, he would place upon his long, yellow locks, his little peaked Forester's hat, with the heron's feather stuck jauntily at one side of it. He would then take from its case his zither —which he played quite as well as he did the harmonica—and prepare for a pleasant Sunday.

One Sunday evening Pete had been playing upon his zither a very sweet air, which he said was a German song. Translated into English, the title was "Over the Hills and Far Away." This tune seemed to Annie very sad. Somehow it brought the tears to the child's eye—she could not tell exactly why,—and it caused Billy, the burro, to burst out into such a wild "he-hawing" of grief, rage and lamentation, that Annie trembled and drew her little chair closer to Pete.

"Oh, don't play that any more, please," she said, "it makes me feel so lonesome."

"That is not a very lively tune," said Pete calmly. "Over in my Hartz country, they believe when you play that tune, it brings the 'Little Hill Folks' up from their homes in the caves of the mountains, to listen to it."

"Are these hill folks so very little, or are they as big as I am?" asked Annie. Pete waited a minute, loosening the strings of his zither before placing it in its case, then said:—

"My cousin Hedwig, who lives near Ilsenburg,—well, once she saw a Little Hill Woman, my cousin said she was as big as a child three years old. My gracious! but she was strong! Hedwig saw her lift a stone so large that no strong man could lift it."

"I wonder what they do all day in their country, away down in the earth," said Annie.

"Well, they are all miners or metal workers; blacksmiths, silversmiths, copper and goldsmiths. They hammer out beautiful swords and knives, and goblets of gold and of silver — all engraved with queer patterns and figures, such as no man on earth can ever make — so strange and so beautiful," said Pete. "Yes, they have a fine life down there, for they are very rich, and have piles of beautiful stones, too; for, of course, they know where the richest gem mines are, as well as the gold mines."

"I do wish they would take a liking to my papa and show him

where to dig for 'pay dirt,'" said Annie.

"But, my Annie," said Pete, "there are many races and people of little folks besides the little brown Gnomes. They always live in mountain countries and down deep under the earth, but the beautiful fairies are the Pixies and the Nixies. The Pixies live in the meadows and woods, and they are very small, so small that they can hide away in the flower cups at the least sign that somebody is near. They are jolly little people and have their regular meeting places in the fields and forests, where they come out to play and dance around in circles, in the moonlight.

"The butterflies know them well and the bees run upon their errands and fur-

nish them with sweets from the purest, fairest flowers.

"The Nixies are water people. They are not so small, but are very beautiful in shape and color. They live on the beds of rivers and streams, in houses of crystal, so clear that one down there can see right through them.

"The old Water Nix sits on the bank and coaxes children to come to him; but alas, for the little girl who lets the old Nix coax her to his side, for he will bind her quickly with the long, green ribbon he has hidden away in the willows, and will draw her down to his crystal palace, there to keep her prisoner for years and years, away from parents and home, with only the fishes and the mermaids—

who are the old Nixie's daughters — to play with."

"I think I like the Gnomes the best of all the fairy folks, even if they are not very pretty," said Annie, with a little shiver. "They are the most like real live people."

"Yes," said Pete, "the Little Hill Folks have good hearts, and they never forget a kindness."

"Well," said Annie, "if ever I am to learn things like Lizzie May and other children, some kind Fairy will have to help my papa to luck pretty soon or I shall grow so big I shall be ashamed to go to school."

"You always talk of school, my Annie," said Pete. "Why, you go to

school every day, little dreamer—to Mother Nature's wonderful school, where all the flowers and birds are your teachers."

"Yes, I know, Pete; but I want to go where there are other children who can talk to me," said Annie

"Ah, my Annie," answered Pete, "everything talks; the flowers and trees talk in their own way. Everything has its own language. Ours is but the work to learn it; learn to watch and listen with your eyes and ears, and heart as well, then you may some day understand a little of the beautiful things that Nature is trying to teach you."

Pete's big, honest blue eyes were beginning to have that dreamy look in

them which Annie knew so well. She also knew that when he looked dreamy, he forgot to answer her questions, and was not a very interesting companion, so she bade him good night and went in to put Arabella in her crib.

That night, tucked up in her little white bed, Annie lay awake for a long time, watching the moonbeams as they stole through the morning glory vines shading her window, and she thought over all she had heard from Pete, of the silent fairy races who live all around us, yet are so quiet that we cannot see them. Then the mystery of the trapped prairie dog came to her mind and she was glad she had been able to help it, for no doubt, she thought, it was a Gnome in disguise, and some day it might show her father the way to the gold mine, and then she would learn everything—even how to dance, like Lizzie May.

For, after hearing Pete talk, it was quite certain that all the wonderful things did not happen in cities. Then Annie's thoughts wandered off to what Professor Pratt had told her about the fossils, up in the Bad Lands; and the Mastodons, and Glyptodons and Pterodactyls. Thinking of these things, Annie fell asleep and dreamed a very vivid dream.

She thought she was down at her play-house, by the creek, having a tea party, with Arabella and Silvertip for guests, when suddenly a queer animal, with web

feet like a duck's and a big mouth like a frog's, climbed up the bank from the mud of the creek and swallowed Silver-tip at one gulp, then Arabella, and then began to chase Annie, herself, around the old willow tree.

She awoke, screaming, to find Marthy Stubbs shaking her by the shoulder, and asking what on earth was the matter. "Oh, Marthy," whimpered Annie, "I'm so glad you came, that old Fossil was after me, it was the Pterodactyl, I guess, it was awful."

"Terry, nonsense," said Marthy crossly. "Why, you've waked up every-body in the house, yelling like a wild Indian. What crazy thing won't you dream of next? If I was your grandma

I wouldn't ever let you look at those old books Professor Pratt left here, with their horrid pictures, such a nervous child as you are. There, I'll lie along side of you till morning, if you will shut your eyes and go to sleep and sleep decent, like other folks."

Chapter V
Annie's Seventh Birthday

IT WAS June, and everything was looking its best, out in South Dakota. It was a glorious time of year, and Annie was looking forward to her seventh birthday, with the feeling that it was surely going to bring about some happy change in her life. It now wanted just one week to that time, the 21st of June.

One day Pete brought home from the distant town, a big gay colored hand bill, telling of the circus that was coming to town. It was to stop for one day at Cave City, and as that day was to be the 21st of June, Annie thought what a delight it would be to go to the show with Pete. She thought that it must be one of the greatest shows on earth, from the gay pictures on the hand bills. These showed every kind of strange animal one could think of, lions and tigers, elephants, striped zebras, etc. Even more wonderful were the lady riders, dashing through big hoops held in air by splendidly dressed ring masters and then alighting on white horses and galloping on, around and around the ring.

Annie, who had never been to a show in all her life, could scarcely sleep nights

now for thinking about it, and her grandmother had consented to let her go.

Time dragged slowly on. It was the day before the 21st, when old Jeff suddenly fell lame. He had stepped upon a sharp stone and hurt his foot. The circus had to be given up.

It was a cruel disappointment, and to comfort her, her grandmother said she should go to town with her the following week, but, alas, that would not be on her birthday.

It is a very wonderful thing to be just seven years old. Annie tried not to grieve over her disappointment, but felt that she could not bear much more.

The morning of June 21st dawned clear and bright, the dew still sparkled on the grass when the little girl, taking Arabella under her arm and her sun bonnet from its nail, with a small tin pail from the pantry shelf, started off without saying a word to anyone as to where she was going. As she passed by the barn her cat got up from a rat hole he was watching and came bounding after her.

Annie hurried through the kitchen garden, where the rows of cabbages and onions and heads of lettuce were looking thrifty, and where the tall hollyhocks and sunflowers were lifting up their great flowers to the kiss of the Eastern light.

Then she crawled through a hole in the fence, and came out into a field of

wheat and through that into the pasture where the cows were just breakfasting off green grass and dandelions. At last her little brown feet struck the foot path that led down to the creek, but before she came to the creek itself, which flowed in many a winding turn through the McLane farm, she had to go through some low marsh land. Annie loved to go through this spot, for it was a little world all by itself, different in every way from the prairie. Here grew broad leaved water plants, tall reeds and jointed bulrushes and the fluer-de-lis, with its sweet scent and lovely blue and yellow blossoms.

Here among the tall grasses grew wild mint and pennyroyal, making the air spicy with their fragrance. Here frogs hopped about and the water fowls built nests, and dragon flies with wings of rainbow gauze darted hither and thither, and big bumble bees came to rifle the blossoms, and gorgeous butterflies sailed lazily, fanning the flowers with their great gay colored wings, and at night the fireflies danced their merry dance over it until the morning.

Yet this morning, as the little girl wandered on, swinging her tin pail listlessly, with her sun bonnet falling back from her chubby, freckled face, she did not seem to notice everything as usually she did, and there was a sad expression in her big blue eyes that always looked about so full of wonder and interest.

This morning she never stopped once to pull the joints from the bulrush, or pick up one of the small shells that lay thickly around, or call Silvertip away from his too close examination of a nest full of young meadow larks.

It was the 21st of June, Annie's seventh birthday, a day she had looked forward to for months, thinking that she would surely celebrate it in some new and delightful way, either by a party, or going to town, or doing something quite out of the common.

Yet, as is often the way, when one has long looked forward to a pleasant time, everything had gone wrong with Annie that June morning. It had begun the minute she was out of bed.

When she combed her hair, it snarled up, caught in the comb and pulled and hurt her so, that it brought tears to her eyes.

When she went down stairs, the first news she heard was, that her grandmother was sick in bed with one of her bad headaches, and Annie could see there was not the very faintest hope of any birthday cake from Marthy Stubbs, who was cross because the day was hot and she would have the work to do all alone.

When Annie took Arabella out of her crib to dress her, she found that some way or other the old doll had sprung a leak in her left side and that every time she was moved the saw dust poured out of her.

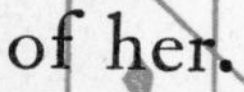

Everybody seemed to have entirely forgotten that this was Annie McLane's birthday and that she was now seven years old. Even Pete, who never before had forgotten to give her some little present on Christmas and her birthday, even Pete had gone off to see the show at Cave City, he had gone early that morning, in the wagon with Nils Nilson and his eight tow-headed children. This was hard to bear.

To cap the climax, when the little girl went out to feed her pets, she found that Captain Gib had been fighting Pantallettes. The poor little white rooster was all covered with blood and nearly dead. Annie parted them and gave Captain Gib a good thrashing.

Then, utterly worn out with the morning's trials, she sat down back of the chicken house and wept long and bitterly. Arabella, Pantallettes and Silvertip grouped around her, looked on pityingly and wondered what could be the matter with their little mistress, who was usually so cheerful and gay. Certainly this was not a very bright beginning for one's birthday.

When Annie had cried until her eyes were red and her head ached terribly, she resolved to rush away from a house where no one seemed to take any interest in her affairs.

Then she remembered that it was about the time for the wild strawberries to be ripe and concluded to take her little pail along and perhaps gather a few for her grandmother's tea that evening.

To make everything seem darker by contrast, the evening before the 21st a letter had come to them from Aunt Molly, and among other things, she described a beautiful French doll that had just been presented to Lizzie May. It was a remarkable doll and could open and shut its eyes.

Now, usually, Annie was extremely gentle with Arabella, but somehow, this morning, the impassive stare on the homely old rag doll's face maddened her. "Stop looking like that, you poor silly thing!" she said, shaking Arabella. "Why don't you open and shut your eyes? you can't, you know you can't—

you never did have any sense, anyhow, and now you had to go and tear a big hole in your side, just on my birthday, too."

Of course, such treatment as this only made the poor old doll leak worse than ever, and this, too, was irritating. Annie grew quite reckless now, and carried Arabella by one leg, with her head hanging down. A cruel way to treat a patient old doll, but the little girl was out of harmony with the peace and beauty all around her.

She did not realize it, but it was really she, Annie McLane herself, who was making all this unhappiness by her own bitter and discontented thoughts. For thoughts are real things, even if you cannot see them, and their effects can always be seen. It is by thinking bad thoughts that children—the big as well as the little ones—make themselves and all surrounding them miserable.

The first thing that happened to take Annie's thoughts far away from herself and her troubles was this singular incident: When she came to the place on the creek bank, right opposite her playhouse, under the old willow tree, where a board is put across for a foot bridge, she looked up and saw, near the playhouse, three water wagtails, all sitting in a row, on a tall alder bush that leaned over the water.

This interested her at once, for Pete Pumpernickel had often said that

when you saw three water wagtails sitting in a row, it was a sure sign that something strange, unusual and quite out of the common was going to happen, and so, who could tell, perhaps, her birthday was going to be different from common days after all. She earnestly hoped so.

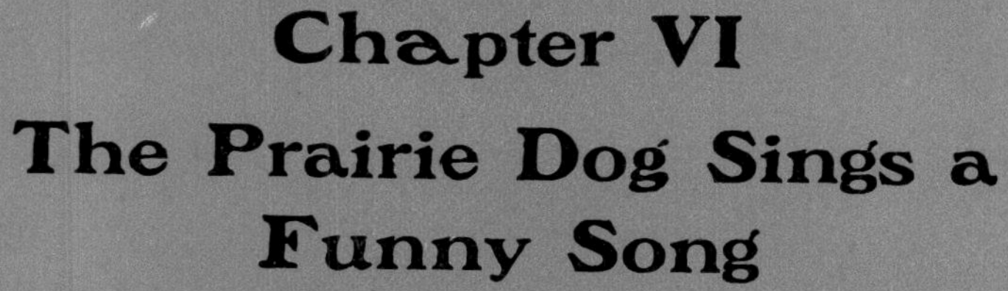

Chapter VI

The Prairie Dog Sings a Funny Song

The DEW still glittered on the grass when Annie found the sunny bank on the side of the creek where the strawberries grew, and set to work to fill her little tin pail with them. As she worked the sweet smell of the mint and flowers and the morning song of the meadow larks, who were calling to each other all over the prairies; all of these pleasant things stole into the child's heart and soothed her.

As usual she fell to thinking of the Pixies, Gnomes and Nixies, Witches and Charms, of Pete's stories and imagining what she would say to the King of the Little Hill Men, if she could see him.

As she thought, she kept on picking the red, juicy berries, and so earnestly was she thinking that almost before she knew it, her little brown hand would carry them straight up to her little rosy mouth.

At last she kept tasting them and tasting them, until she had eaten up every berry and there were no more patches to be found, and it was nearly dinner time.

The little girl was very tired and hot, so, following the windings of the creek,

she came to the old willow tree and sat down to rest and bathe her dusty little feet in the cool water. As she did so, she noticed the three water wagtails, who were acting in the queerest way, flying around and around in circles, then lighting on the alder bush, and flirting water from their tails and wings.

She watched them earnestly, for it seemed as though they were trying to tell her something, or show her something, they were so excited, and always doing the same thing over and over, flying low, in a circle. The sunbeams, that were playing hide and seek with the little minnows in the clear water, must have taken Annie's eyes for

blue forget-me-not flowers, for they shone into them and dazzled them. The little girl closed her eyes to rest them for a minute. It seemed to her that no sooner were her eyes closed than she was startled by hearing, sung in a rather squeaky voice, the words of the following curious song:

"In the new of the moon,
By a clear running stream,
If you should chance to fall asleep,
Be careful what you dream.
For if you will not take advice,
Your course you'll surely rue,
In the lovely land of Lollipops
Where dreams come true.

By a clear flowing stream--
Please take notice what I say:--
Every naughty thought you think
Will open up a way,

For the hoblins and goblins
  To come riding on the gales,
With nits and gnats and buzzy things
  With stingers in their tails.

Oh, once there was a little girl
  Who snarled and cried and whined,
She twisted round her face so much,
  At last it grew behind,
So let your face be smiling
  And your thoughts be pleasant too,
When you seek the land of Lollipops,
  Where dreams come true."

Annie was so surprised she dropped Arabella into the creek and the empty tin pail fell from her hands and went floating down stream after the poor doll, who was soon out of sight. There was a pang of grief in Annie's heart when she saw the last of the old doll as it whirled around a big boulder, but the

strange voice puzzled her so that she could think of nothing else.

Looking around her, no human being was in sight. She rubbed her eyes. What could it all mean? Was she bewitched? This was certainly very much like one of Pete's stories.

It could not be the water wagtails; they were flying about as they had been before she closed her eyes.

Suddenly, looking down, a few steps away from her, on a little clay hillock, she saw a rather large prairie dog, sitting up in a very straight, military fashion on his haunches and watching her face, while he stroked his whiskers with his left paw.

"Excuse me, Miss," he said, bowing in a very polite manner, "I really did

not intend to startle you." "But, you did startle me, so that I dropped my doll and she will be drowned," said Annie, sharply. She had always had a poor opinion of prairie dogs since that one with the crushed paw had run away from her, without the least sign of gratitude.

"I am truly sorry," said the prairie dog, as he stooped down and pulled some mint and began munching it.

"Was that you singing just a minute ago?" Annie enquired eagerly. "Yes," said the prairie dog, "I was humming a little song, very popular just now with us. Everything is singing to-day and it is hard to keep from joining in with the birds and the bees and the running water."

"But what funny words those were," said Annie. "Oh," replied the prairie dog, "There is no one in our country, who does not know of the land where dreams come true, and as to thoughts, why good gracious! they are really the only things that last forever."

"I should dearly love to see that country," said Annie, thoughtfully. "Is it a long way from here?"

"Well, I suppose I could start you on the road to-day, only if once you are started you must keep right on, and not get tired and frightened. You seem a nice little girl, so I am willing to grant you any favor in my power, should you wish to leave your home; but you surely have everything to make you happy here, if you only would think so."

"Oh," said Annie, her eyes full of tears and a sob in her voice, "I am very, very lonesome, and I don't think I have any friends who love me very much, for I am seven years old to-day, and everybody seems to have forgotten all about it and I never, never was at a show in all my life, and they would not let me go, and I am getting to be so old and have never been to school, and—and"—Here all Annie's sorrows came over her, in a big black cloud of despair, and she buried her face in her hands and for the second time that day, cried bitterly.

"My stars!" said the prairie dog,—"Well, this is a pretty state of affairs.

Don't cry so,—here let me take your hand." "What for," said Annie,—shrinking from his funny little paw. "Oh, I only want to tell your fortune," said he.

Annie gave him her little brown hand, and he peered into it a long time turning it this way and that. At last he began to speak very seriously and Annie dried her tears to hear what was in store for her in the future.

"I see in this hand," said the prairie dog, "A life of adventure and travel. I see also by these lines, that up to the present, your life has been a very happy one, in fact, the very happiest life a child could have. You have had freedom, fresh air, the company of the flowers, and the animals and birds and butter-

flies, Mother Nature's children, like yourself." "Yet," here he fixed his sharp, gleaming, black eyes steadily upon Annie's face, "Yet, like all mortals, you do not appreciate the blessings of the present, but are always longing for the future." Bending his face lower over the little hand, he went on; "I see that you have had bitter, envious, and discontented thoughts this morning." Annie's eyes fell before his searching gaze.

"Ah, ha," he cried, grasping her hand in his little paw so tightly that she winced,—"So you are a greedy little girl, you ate up all the strawberries."

Annie's face blushed crimson, evidently this dreadful creature knew all one's secret thoughts and actions. She

tried to pull her hand away from his clutch.

"You think you have a kind heart, and yet you could forget all about your good old grandmother, when you know how fond she is of wild strawberries."

"Well," said the little girl, almost crying, "I did not mean to do it, indeed I did not. At first I just tasted one little one, to see if they were ripe, then I got thinking and kept on tasting and tasting until, when I looked down into my little pail, there weren't any left, at all, and I looked around a long time to find another patch, but the sun was so hot and my feet ached so, I just sat down to cool them in the creek."

"How did you know I ate up all the

berries?"—To tell the truth there were berry stains all around Annie's mouth. "Oh, I am something of a mind reader," answered the prairie dog, with a rather mysterious smile. This was growing serious.

"Well, I do think it just dreadfully mean," Annie went on, "that always the very nicest things should be so scarce and put up in such little stingy bunches. Now, there are pumpkins, no one cares much about them, except cows, yet see how big they grow. Oh, I wish I could find some wild strawberries that grew as big as pumpkins, then there would be a chance to have a strawberry short cake that would go around, when there was company to dinner."

No sooner had Annie spoken this wish aloud, than the water wagtails began to squawk and flutter around her as though in great fear and distress, while the prairie dog acted pleased and said: "That's right, that's right, keep right on, I do love to hear people wish aloud. Now maybe you might have a few other nice, sensible wishes like this last one, if so, why speak right out. Don't be bashful before me, I'm only a little prairie dog, who don't know much and who has had to dig for every bit of knowledge he has. Ha-ha-ha-ha-ha-."

His laughter was not pleasant, yet somehow Annie felt that politeness required her to laugh too, so, although she was terribly frightened at this queer

creature, she said, "Ha-ha-ha-ha-ha," too. In the meantime her companion had drawn from under his forearm a tiny cube like a seal, and pressing it upon Annie's little wrist, he said with a smirk, "There, Miss, I just sealed wish number one."

She saw a little round red circle appear on her wrist. She then heard these words in her ear, seemingly from the water wagtails:—

"In the new of the moon,
When the cowslips are in flower,
To sit beneath a willow tree,
Will give the fairies power.
If you wish three times aloud,
While the dew is on the grass,
The charm will work, for good or ill,
Your wish will come to pass."

Everything was growing queerer and queerer. Annie knew in a dim hazy way that the birds sang this as a kind of warning to her, against the prairie dog, but he kept his sharp eyes on her in such a way that she could not leave him

Then she said: "Oh, I do wish that my papa would strike 'pay dirt' soon, and I wish I could see some one who could tell me things I want to know. I think I'd like to see even a Witch, if she knew ever so much and would answer my questions."

"Ha-ha-ha-ha," said the prairie dog, "why, you are a child after my own heart. Let me take your wrist,—one, two, three, yes, you made three wishes. Well, here are the seals of them," and he

made two more little round red marks on Annie's wrist.

Here the water wagtails gave a wild cry of fear and flew away.

With a grin on his face but with a low bow, the prairie dog said: "Miss, now you are initiated into our Order and have taken the first degree, as is shown by these marks on your wrist.

"I cannot stay with you longer to-day, but, rest assured, we shall meet again. In the meantime, Miss, let me advise you to turn your attention to your cat, he seems to be suffering."

Annie turned around and there stood Silvertip, his tail all swelled up to three times its usual size, his back hunched up, his eyes bulging out, his mouth open and

his jaws rigid. As Annie looked at him, in great distress, suddenly he collapsed completely and lay limp and fainting at the feet of his little mistress.

Chapter VII

Annie is taken to the Gnome King's Palace

Annie DRAGGED Silvertip—who still lay in a fit—to the edge of the creek, and stood looking at him, and wringing her hands.

"Oh, poor Silvertip," she cried, "don't you die, and leave me alone." Then there was a rush of wings and she saw that the three friendly water wagtails had come back, and one of them had brought in its beak a sprig of catnip

and hopping up to the fainting cat, held it close to his nose.

Another one of them flirted water into Silvertip's face from the creek with its wings, while the third flew around her head, chirping these words:

"Hush your crying Annie dear,
Your cat is only faint from fear,
But as soon as he revives,
Run, oh run, for both your lives,
Run, and pause not on your way.
The Gnome King walks abroad to-day."

Annie turned to where a minute before, the prairie dog had stood, there was nothing there but a big bumble bee sucking the honey from a blue flag flower.

The prairie dog had vanished and, strangest of all, the hole in the ground

out of which he had so mysteriously popped, was gone too.

This last discovery settled it all in Annie's mind, she knew now that she had been talking with a being from Fairyland, for where was there ever a common prairie dog or gopher that could vanish in such a manner?

Then she remembered Pete's stories about how the Gnome King coaxed little children down into his dim under world sometimes and kept them there, away from parents and friends for years and years.

She picked up her cat, which had revived a little, and ran as fast as she could. As she ran she saw, a little way ahead of her and out of her path, a

bunch of the tallest reddest lilies she had ever seen in all her life. They were moving in the wind, and, frightened though she was, Annie, in spite of the water wagtail's warning, stopped to gather them.

With her eyes upon the beautiful red flowers Annie did not see that her feet were nearing what looked like a big rabbit hole, until she was right on the edge of it, then it was too late. Just as she would have jumped over it, a great big gust of wind came up out of it.

In another minute, she felt the wind lift her off her feet, and she was sucked down, down, what seemed to her, miles, under the ground.

She tried to scream, but the roaring wind took her breath away. In despair and with a last loving thought of her dear father and grandmother and Pete, the little girl closed her eyes and gave herself up for lost.

Annie never knew how long she had been unconscious, but she was awakened by a tinkling sound, as of water running over stones. She opened her eyes and looked wonderingly about her.

She was lying upon a bed of dry moss, in what seemed to be a large cave. It looked much like the description Annie had heard Professor Phineas Pratt give of Wind Cave, which was not very far from her home.

It was cool down there, and the light was dim, but she could see long, glittering things hanging from the lofty roof overhead, where tiny lights gleamed here and there, like stars. A little brook ran close beside her.

Feeling dizzy and queer, she arose and went to get a drink of water from it. As she stooped, something touched her on the shoulder and looking up, she saw at her side, the queerest, quaintest looking little man she had ever seen or fancied, even in her dreams. He was dressed in brown, with an odd peaked cap on his head, which looked much too big for his body, which was about the size of a three year old child. He carried a big hammer in one hand and

the handle was all beautifully carved and the hammer part glistened like burnished copper.

"Oh, where am I?" cried little Annie, "and who are you? Where is that dreadful prairie dog? I've felt so funny ever since he made those queer red marks on my wrists, that I don't really know if I am myself, or somebody else. I used to be Annie McLane, but now I feel just like one of those enchanted princesses Pete used to tell me about."

The queer little man seemed dumb, for he would not answer her in words, but put his finger on his lips, then pointed to the wall. Something dark and soft hung on it by a golden nail

—everything was gold and silver about this place.

Annie felt of it. It was a prairie dog's skin. She looked at the little man, who never smiled or moved a muscle of his face. Then she sank again on the moss, overcome, for she saw that she had been carried off down here through the magic arts of the Gnome King, who had her in his power now. He had worn the animal skin as a disguise.

It was a dreadful shock to her. She was overcome with loneliness and fright. She felt that she must scream and cry out but just then something soft touched her. It was Silvertip, licking her hand. This little touch of sympathy

comforted her wonderfully. She caught her faithful cat in her arms and covered him with kisses. "Oh, my poor cat," cried Annie. "We must help and comfort each other." "Miaow, miaow," said Silvertip.

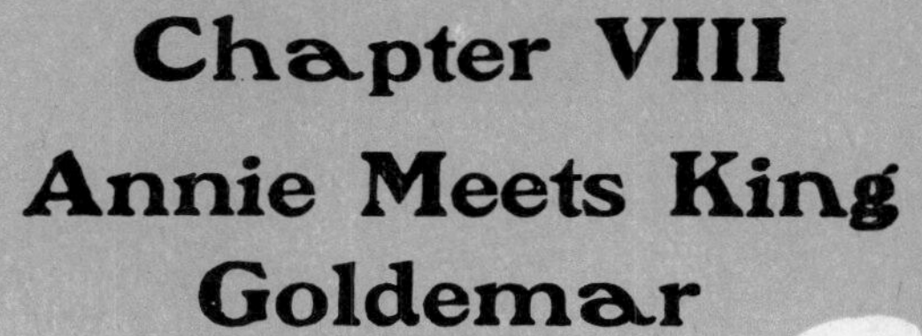

Chapter VIII
Annie Meets King Goldemar

After THE little girl had cried and Silvertip had shown his sympathy by purring in her ear, and rubbing against her, she drank some of the clear cold water of the stream and washed her face and hands in it.

Annie leaned her head down upon Silvertip's soft warm fur, and tried to think earnestly which direction she had better take to find her way out into the sunlight again.

While she bent over Silvertip, making her plans to get away, some one touched her on the shoulder. Annie looked up. The Little Hill Man stood before her. He looked into her eyes very steadily, but his expression was kind. He did not speak, but beckoned her to follow him.

Hope sprang up in the tired frightened girl's heart, for she thought that the Gnome pitied her, and was going to lead her back safely home, to light and liberty. Oh, how dear to her now seemed that little brown house on the prairie, which only this morning she had been glad to get away from, and thought so lonesome and poor a place.

How sorry she felt for all her bad, discontented thoughts. How happy seemed the careless free life she had led, with its pets and friends and everyday tasks.

Holding Silvertip closely in her arms, she followed her strange guide. On they walked through what seemed, at least, a mile of narrow, rocky passage way. It seemed to be leading them down deeper into the earth, for the ground was always slanting in the direction they were traveling.

Her guide had lighted a queer little round lantern, and the bells around his peaked high hat tinkled musically at every step he took. Annie saw many beautiful things on this her first journey in the Under World.

On either hand, from the walls and roof were hanging beautiful crystals of every form and color. Here she saw what appeared to be a cluster of the brightest diamonds. There were rubies and sapphires; just beyond, near the floor, were thousands of emeralds.

At one place Annie thought she had found a veritable candy room, for hanging from the walls were hundreds of white and colored crystals, which looked like sticks of candy growing right out of the roof of the cave.

Again they passed through a perfect net work of crystals, which reminded one of myriads of petrified cobwebs set with drops of frozen dew. Just beyond was a chamber of petrified honey combs,

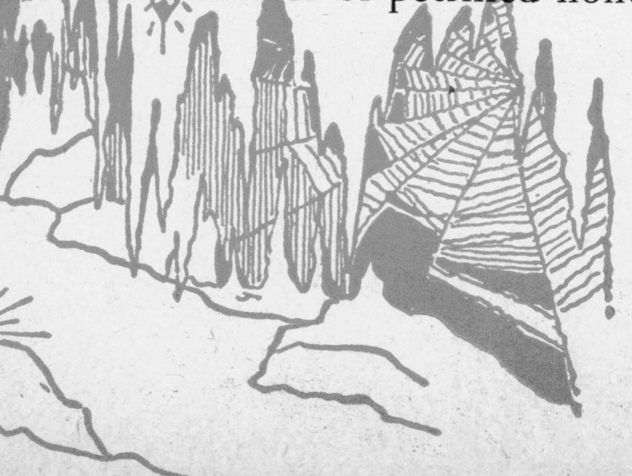

all bright and shiny, which gave every tone of the cathedral bells, when accidently struck by the staff of the little guide.

One place in particular so enchanted Annie that she forgot all her troubles. This was a fairy bride's chamber. Here, just before her and on her left, she saw a brilliantly lighted room of splendid design and purest crystal. From the walls and ceiling, myriads of tiny needles, stars, triangles and crosses of every kind and color, were suspended and every article, couch, settee, mirror, chairs and footstools were set with brilliant gems, which shone and glistened in the hidden colored lights like a hundred sunsets and a thousand rainbows. But, most

wonderful of all, right in front of them and suspended from the ceiling, hung what looked like a beautiful and delicately woven lace curtain, all set with diamonds, rubies and sapphires.

This wonderful curtain partly cut off the view of the bride's chamber, but it was so filmy and delicate that Annie could scarcely believe it was all made of tiny mineral threads and crystal gems.

As they journeyed on and on, they saw many other wonderful things, but they had far to go and could not stop to examine everything.

"Oh, dear me, I am so dreadfully tired, and so hungry too, and thirsty," cried Annie. "Are not we almost home?"

Her guide shook his head, then he motioned for her to sit down on a boulder that partly blocked up the narrow road. Annie sank down glad to rest a minute.

The Gnome pulled a small gold flask from his pocket, unscrewed the top, which was now a little cup with jewels around the rim, and poured out some milk, which he gave Annie to drink. It was delicious sweet milk and she drank two or three cups of it and gave some to Silvertip.

The Gnome also gave her some little cakes, which tasted very nice; they were thin, and round, and small, and were sweetened with honey, and there were nuts in them, and some delicious spicy seeds, a very little like the carraway Annie's grandmother put in cookies, only nicer.

She felt much refreshed after her little rest, and so they went on again, but Annie had now given up all hope that the Gnome was taking her home.

The guide finally took a silver whistle from his pocket and blew upon it three times. Noiselessly, the wall in front of them opened. They saw before them a long and lofty hall brilliantly lighted, with colored lamps in rows all around the ceiling.

Annie could not keep from crying out, "Oh, how beautiful," as she stepped into this room and looked about her.

All around, in corners and down the

sides of the hall, were ranged tall vases of silver and gold, full of glittering heaps of flashing jewels of every color that could be imagined.

She wanted to stop longer, but her guide marched on, beckoning her to follow.

Now they came to two massive doors, and her guide touched lightly what seemed to be a silver rose, that jutted out from the center of one of them. The big doors rolled apart, and before them was another large room, beautiful as a dream.

Its walls were all of the purest, clearest crystal, which had been cut into a thousand shapes. These edges and points caught and reflected every ray that came from a great ball of light that hung by diamond chains from the dome of the ceiling. Over these walls there crept hundreds of those beautiful little lizards called chameleons. Each one of the pretty creatures wore upon his head a tiny gold crown, which was set with rubies, emeralds, topazes, sapphires and costly gems of various colors.

As these little creatures crept over the walls, among the crystal leaves and flowers, the lights caught up and reflected the changing colors of their translucent bodies, and their flashing jewelled crowns. They made such a shimmer and shining, and glimmer and glint and gleam, that it was more

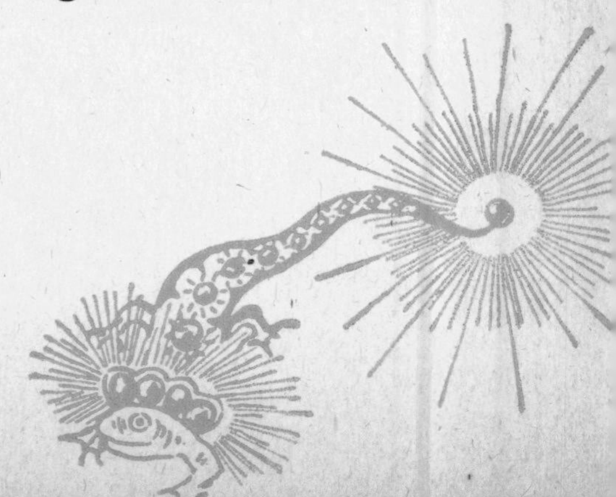

beautiful than even the Dakota sunsets, which Annie had watched many a time, with wondering eyes, thinking each splendid glow of color more beautiful than that which went before.

"Oh, have we come then at last to the end of the Rainbow Road? For surely this must be the palace of the Great Wise Witch, Zauberlinda."

Here, for the first time, her guide seemed to have found his tongue, for he said: "No, this is not Zauberlinda's Palace. You are in the realm of King Goldemar, the ruler of the Gnomes."

Annie scarcely heard him, for she was staring up in wonder at the high ceiling. It was of crystal, so transparent and clear that she at first thought there was no ceiling at all, but just the air of heaven, with blue and gold clouds in it.

Later, she saw that these twisting curling cloud shapes were the most beautiful blue and gold and white serpents, transparent as purest air. They moved all the time, writhing and twisting their slender bodies into ever changing shapes. This ceiling thus became an ever changing, ever beautiful wonder, and every time the cloud like shapes stirred, there followed a strain of music that sounded dream-like and mellow as though it came from far away. This was the only break in the stillness. There were no sounds of talking or laughter of children at play, or song of bird, or hum of insect.

As Annie entered the room, the tiny chameleons on the walls, turned to look at her with such friendly, bright eyes, that she longed to coax one of the pretty little creatures to her, that she might stroke and caress it.

So completely surprised and overcome was the child with all this color, splendor and beauty, that she did not see that her guide was waiting for her to follow him, until he called for her to hurry. She caught up with him and once more the big folding doors noiselessly rolled apart for them and they stepped into the third room.

This was a larger apartment than the first, or the second, and if possible still more beautiful. The walls of this room were made of shining silver ore, and out of them seemed to grow creeping plants and flowers of the prettiest, brightest colors. Annie could not refrain from running up to smell them.

Fancy her disappointment, when she found that these flowers were all artificial, made from costly gems, rubies, sapphires and diamonds—for the gems are the only flowers of the Under World—and with them the cunning Gnomes can imitate earthly flowers so perfectly, that they deceive the sharpest eye—but not the nose. Annie thought she would have given more that very minute, for one good sniff of the old fashioned lilac blossoms that burst out every Spring from the big bush by their gate at

home, than for all these cold, scentless, gorgeous shams.

The room was full of little Gnomes. These were the noblemen who composed the court of King Goldemar. They all looked at her so curiously that Annie felt very bashful and timid. The people were simply dressed, like Annie's guide, and like him, they had earnest, intelligent faces, with clear beaming eyes.

As Annie entered they all took off their odd peaked hats and bowed low.

This was the throne room of the castle. A great golden eagle, with diamond eyes, was fastened by an invisible cord to the ceiling. He held in his bill four diamond chains, which

held up a throne, cut entirely out of one enormous ruby. This throne was cushioned with costly white satin and had the king's seal and coat of arms embroidered upon the center of the back.

A majestic looking monarch was seated on this throne. Although small in stature, he had a lofty dignity about him, and clear, piercing eyes, and such a commanding way with him, that Annie trembled and did not dare to look up.

This was the powerful King of the Gnomes, Goldemar.

His hair and beard gleamed like silver, as they flowed down upon his long crimson velvet mantle.

Annie trembled like a leaf, as they led her before the king, and kept her eyes on the floor.

"Bring this Child of Upper Earth still nearer," she heard him say.

At last she stood alone, upon the first of the steps that led up to his throne. She could hear her own heart beat "thump, thump, thump," while she stood there, a poor little lonely girl, far from home and friends, a stranger indeed in a strange land.

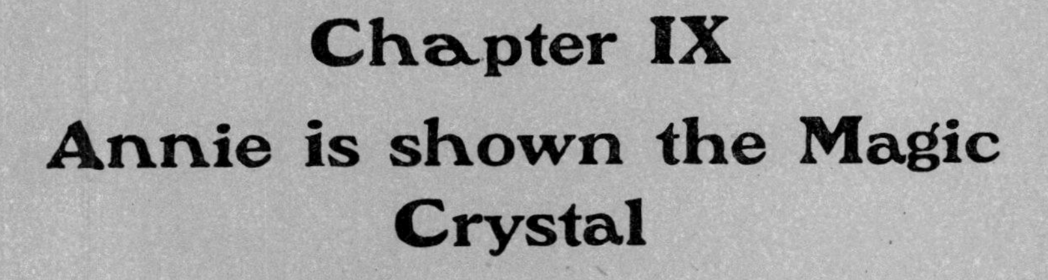

Chapter IX

Annie is shown the Magic Crystal

"Listen CHILD of Upper Earth," said the Gnome King, holding up his hand, upon the fore-finger of which gleamed the great Magic Crystal of his signet ring.

"Know that it is our royal will to confer upon thee, the greatest honor ever offered to Child of Mortal. Would'st thou know the cause for the favor shown thee—then listen. We Gnomes remember well. A kind deed done to our race never yet went unrewarded. No crime against us can long remain unavenged. One year ago to-day, my son, while walking in the fields of Upper Earth, disguised, had the misfortune to have his hand caught in one of those cruel traps made by man.

"You rescued the Royal Prince that day. He walked the fields of Upper Earth disguised as a prairie dog.

"You know the rest, how he was caught, how you opened the cruel trap. He escaped from the home you made for him, for he would soon have pined away and died in your atmosphere.

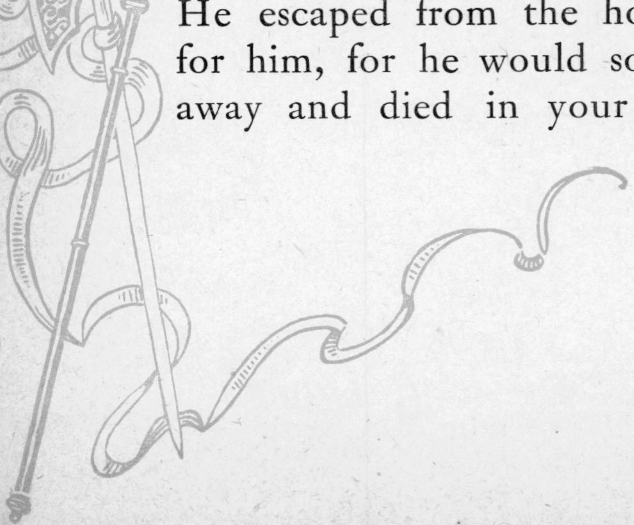

"He returned home, yet, alas, has never been the same since that day. Even as he still bears the mark of the steel teeth of the trap upon his wrist, so does he bear in his heart the trace of a mortal love and sorrow. For, alas, he himself, has a drop of human blood in his veins, it has come down from his mother's race. It makes him weaker, more tender than are we of the pure Gnome ancestry.

"My son escaped and came home, only to talk in his sleep of you; of your goodness and beauty, and to mourn lest you should think him ungrateful because he would not stay to speak, or even look his thanks to you.

"Now, Child Annie, you know why I sent up my wise old ambassador, Grubel, to lure you down to my palace.

"Speak, Child of Earth; ask what you will, it shall be granted you, even to the half of my kingdom."

"Then," said Annie softly, but looking bravely right into the Gnome King's face: "I thank you very much, but as to half of your kingdom, I could not think of accepting it for I would not know what in the world to do with it.

"But, oh! good King Goldemar, I have always wanted to see you, and now I will tell you my wish. It is this: Please let my papa have one streak of good luck. Send one of your little Gnomes to show him the right spot to

dig for rich ore, because when he strikes a gold mine, we shall all be rich, and move to town, and I can go to school." As she grew more and more in earnest, Annie forgot to be timid.

He gazed at her steadily, as though puzzled by her request, and she fancied there was a sneer upon his face as at last he said: "Gold! Gold! Always gold, is what these mortals plead for, and sweat, and toil, and crave for; it seems that even their innocent babes prattle of it.

"Know ye for what you ask fair child? You wish for gold that you may leave the Country for the Town. You ask to exchange the pure air of the hills and prairies for the stifling reek of the cities; water, sparkling up from the crystal springs, the true elixir of life, for the red wine and poisoned potions which bring madness and disease; gauds and shams you will have instead of truth and beauty; care for freedom of spirit; the Worldling's face, a mask of deceit, for eyes that reflect every beautiful emotion of the heart as yonder light flashes back the hues of my rubies and emeralds.

"Know ye not that the bitterness of the curse laid upon us Gnomes lies in the very fact that we are forced to remain down here and forever delve for gold? This it is which makes our faces so sad. We long in vain for

all the simple pleasure you Mortals possess and hold so lightly.

"Alas! our very flowers are of gold and silver and precious stones."

He spoke so sadly, and yet so earnestly, that Annie felt she must explain her reasons for wanting gold, so she said, falteringly: "But I want to learn and grow up to be an educated woman, this is why I wish for Riches, that I may go to school, to wise teachers, who will explain to me all the things that puzzle me so now."

Said the Gnome King: "Child, if you desire to possess knowledge, *that* we can give you, for we have among us scholars, who have studied the Mysteries of Nature for hundreds of years. But

10

Wisdom is something different. Wisdom springs from the heart of Love, and soulless beings can never be illuminated by its beautiful light.

"The most learned scholar of your Upper Earth, never yet attained to the wisdom that lies deep as a fountain in the loving heart of an innocent child like yourself. But your wish shall be granted. Look well at this!" Here he took from his finger the ring, and held it up for Annie to gaze upon. Its setting was a simple stone, flat and oval in shape, colorless as glass, until held up and then a clear ray of greenish light, mellow as moon beams streamed out from it, so that it was much more beautiful than a diamond;

but the light from it was not so glittering but softer, steadier and clearer.

"This Magic Crystal in my signet ring," said Goldemar, "has the power of showing to him who gazes into it, every vein of ore, every mine of gems, clear down to the very center of earth. Therefore, he who has the use of this ring, for but a little while, may easily become rich beyond the wildest dream of mortal.

"Knowing this, every Prince of Fairy Land has envied me this Crystal.

"Your father shall have the use of the Magic Crystal for one year and a day, on one condition—"

"Oh, thank you! thank you! good King Goldemar," cried Annie, kneeling

down to kiss the King's crimson mantle. "Hold!" cried the King. "Do not interrupt, Child of Earth, your father will gain wealth untold, but *you* shall stay with *us* and become the bride of Prince Kuno, my only son.

"You desire Knowledge and Gold; you can have them both here, in more abundance than you could possess them on the Upper Earth."

Annie felt sick and dizzy with terror and disappointment. Such a great wave of homesickness came over her that she could scarcely speak.

Clasping her hands together pleadingly, she said: "Oh, no! no! King Goldemar, I must go back home. Why, my papa would not care at all to find a

gold mine, if he lost his little girl. He is only hunting for it so that he can educate me, and have me learn how to play the piano. He does not need much money for himself, just enough to get a new hat and a pair of boots once in a while and to pay Pete Pumpernickel his wages."

"Child, do you then refuse the honor of becoming the bride of Prince Kuno?" said the Gnome King in a stern voice.

"Yes, I know it is a great honor, and I thank you," said Annie—and now the tears welled up in her eyes, and began pouring down over her cheeks and dropping off the end of her nose and chin—"but please, please, let me go back to the old farm, and you keep your Magic Crystal. I don't want to be rich, and I don't know as I care much about being educated. I see now that there are things in life so much better than riches or learning. I'll study the multiplication table, and learn what I can at home with grandmother. I may have to grow up ignorant, but I can be loving and kind, and oh, that is best of all! I never knew before how dreadfully lonesome any one can be, even with people and pretty things all around.

"Oh dear me! it aches so here," said Annie, putting her little hand on her heart, while great sobs swelled up in her throat until they almost choked her.

She wiped away the blinding tears, with a corner of her little blue and white checked apron, and as she did so, saw for the first time all the little Gnomes crowding closely around her and saying, "Oh!" and "Ah!" and nodding their heads, and making motions to one another, and staring and rolling their eyes, and then peering and pointing at her. Suddenly a little Gnome page ran to a cabinet full of beautiful cups and jeweled vases, and taking a blue vase of solid turquoise, he hurried back and kneeling down held it up under Annie's chin, to catch the tears that still were running down her cheeks.

The earnest faces of the little folks, and the queer act of the Gnome page,

all at once struck Annie's sense of humor so keenly that, even in the midst of her troubles, she burst out laughing.

Such a sound as this, the laughter of a child, had never before been heard in these beautiful rooms. The Gnomes looked anxiously up at the stern face of their King.

"Grubel!" called King Goldemar. Little Grubel, the same wizened old Gnome who had brought Annie to this castle, stepped out from the crowd.

"Grubel, take this girl away, let her be guarded well, but kindly treated, call Mop to entertain her."

Chapter X

Annie Sees the Court Goblin

WHOS MOP," asked Annie, as old Grubel led her out of the throne room, and down a narrow, dark passage. "Mop? Oh, he's the Court Goblin. He is not a Gnome at all, but a Pixey and used to belong to the Great Zauberlinda. We captured him one day and keep him to amuse the King."

"Oh, I see, he's a prisoner, the same as I am," said Annie.

"He's a lively fellow and a wonderful conjuror. There is simply no end to the tricks he can do."

"And Grubel," Annie went on,—she began to feel quite at home with him,—"What made them all peer at me so curiously, and why did that little fellow bring a blue vase and hold it under my chin?"

"It was your weeping, my little lady," said old Grubel. "The people had never seen any one weep before, they wanted to catch your tears and examine them, to see what they were made of."

"How very happy you must be then, since you have never seen any one weep,

and don't know the meaning of tears," said Annie thoughtfully, "but," she added, to herself, "somehow you don't look happy."

"Happy?" repeated old Grubel. "Oh, I don't know, you may have noticed that while you see no one weeping, here, on the other hand no one laughs either. You see, my little lady, the laughter and the tears always lie closely beside each other, like the sunshine and the rain."

"Oh?" said the little child, "It must be a dreadful life, where you never laugh out loud. I will take the tears along with the laughter, I think, and after all, while crying makes your eyes ache it does seem to draw away that

pain at the heart. But, oh! Grubel, when am I to go home, please?"

"My little lady, you had best make up your mind to be contented, for you will spend the rest of your days down here with us," said Grubel.

"But I am only a little girl, Grubel. I am too young to marry anybody."

"They will keep you down here until you are grown," said her guide.

"Besides," Annie went on, "if I ever marry any one, I must marry Pete Pumpernickel. He has promised to wait for me until I am a young lady, he means to be rich by that time, and we have planned our wedding trip. We are going over to Germany to visit his old father and mother."

Old Grubel shrugged his shoulders and nodded his head, then he said: "My little lady, if ever you escape from the palace of the powerful King Goldemar, you will do what no prisoner of his has ever done before."

"Well," said Annie, "I have made up my mind what to do; when young Prince Kuno comes from hunting, I shall go to him and beg him to show me some way out of here and into the upper air again. He is young, like me, and he will feel sorry for me and help me to get back home, I am sure. But if he does not, then I shall tell King Goldemar, that he may keep my body down here if he wants to, but if he does I shall die of a broken heart, so he will lose me

after all, and I shall go to my dear mother in heaven, for the Gnome King has no power over my soul."

"No," said Grubel, "the Gnomes have no souls nor power over souls."

"As they talked they kept on walking down one narrow passage-way and up another. They were now at the entrance of the Chamber of the Court Goblin. Annie and the Gnome entered a little eight cornered room, with red curtains hung across the middle of it. These curtains were suddenly drawn back on either side and showed a little table standing in the center of the room.

"Mop! Mop!" called Grubel. Annie looked toward the door, expecting the conjurer to come in.

What was her surprise, when a little Goblin dropped down on the table from the ceiling, turned six summersaults, then jumped up and ran to the front of the table, bowed and kissed his hand to Annie.

Mop was very small. His legs were crooked and seemed much too slender to carry his head and shoulders. His head was bald as a little gourd. His twinkling eyes were like small black beads, but full of mischief. His mouth was big and wide, with a comical grin upon it. Funny little pointed ears grew out on each side of his round head, near the top of it. His arms and legs were quite long and had hair on them. He wore a little sleeveless shirt, which came down to his knees.

The little Gnome assistant then brought a beautiful jeweled pipe and Annie thought he was going to smoke, a queer thing, surely, for a Goblin to do, but the assistant brought a little basin and a pink cake. The Goblin placed some water in the basin and stirred the cake around in it. Annie saw it was soap, for it made a lot of foaming suds. When it seemed just right to Mop, he began to blow bubbles, and such bubbles as they were, the little girl had never imagined could be blown.

They were of the most gorgeous colors, changing every instant as you looked at them. Somehow they did not seem so fragile as bubbles usually are, for they lasted and floated all around

the room; they danced up and down or around in a circle, at Mop's command.

The room at last was quite full of soap bubbles, for Mop kept on blowing them. When he waved his hand, the shining things floated to him. He threw back his head and began to juggle with them so skillfully, that six of them were kept dancing in the air at the same time. All at once he stopped, stamped his feet and cried, "Piff! paff! puff!" Instantly all the bubbles rose up to the ceiling and burst with a loud report, while a cloud of butterflies, yellow and pink and green, fluttered about for a minute, then flew out of the door.

"My! but he is wonderful," said Annie, with a long breath.

"Oh, that is nothing to what he can do; he's sulky to-day. He pines for the open air and the woods and fields."

"I don't blame him, for so do I," sighed the child.

"Some of our people were hunting night moths last midsummer night, they saw this little fellow sitting in the moonlight, all by himself, on a mullein stalk. He was holding a drop of dew up on a wild rose petal and making faces into it, just for his own amusement. He fought them all he could, but they captured him and now he amuses the court."

"Come, you must see our workshops, for we are really the only hard working inhabitants of Pix-Sylvania." At this, Mop hopped off the table,—he was as nimble as a squirrel,—trotted up to Annie, and held out his little hand with something in it. She took from him a tiny egg, very small like a humming bird's. Mop motioned her to hold it gently in her closed hand. Presently, she felt a tapping inside of the egg. A little young bird was hatching out, and soon had pecked away the thin shell. It was a beautiful downy little thing, not as big as a bee. She would like to have kept it, but Mop came up and taking it tenderly, put it away somewhere.

"Oh, how can he do such wonderful things?" cried Annie.

"He learned his magic from Zauberlinda," answered Grubel. "She can do many wonderful things. She settles the disputes of the birds and animals. She keeps her eye on the weather, and calls the spring flowers up into the light. She puts her magic cipher on the butterflies' wings, and measures the cells of the honey combs for the bees, so they shall be exact and of the regular form. She offers a yearly prize to the sweetest singer among the song birds; the swiftest swimmer among the fish; the prettiest dancer among the Sand Hill Cranes, and the best leaper among the Green Jumpers." "Is she young?" asked Annie.

"Yes," said Grubel, "and beautiful and joyous. She is the special protector of all the wild creatures; they call her the Wise Witch Zauberlinda."

Here Mop came up and laid three small, brown beech-nuts in Annie's hands. She would have given them back, but he jabbered something and shook his head.

"He says they are a gift to you; they are wishing-nuts, and you are to keep them," said old Grubel. "Come, my little lady, to our workshop."

Chapter XI
The Gnome King's Smithy
Meeting the Prince

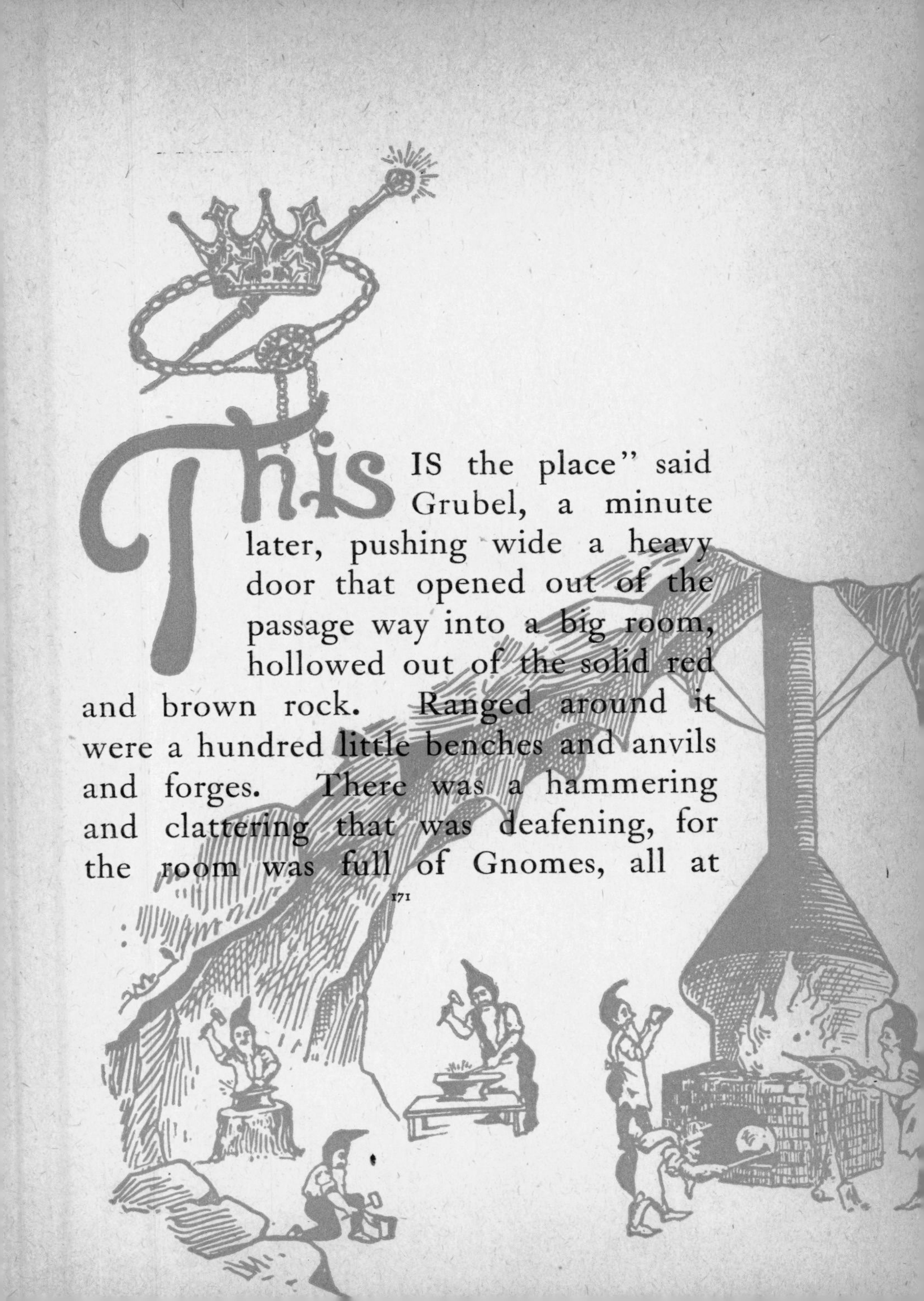

This IS the place" said Grubel, a minute later, pushing wide a heavy door that opened out of the passage way into a big room, hollowed out of the solid red and brown rock. Ranged around it were a hundred little benches and anvils and forges. There was a hammering and clattering that was deafening, for the room was full of Gnomes, all at work. The sturdy little fellows had their sleeves rolled up, their aprons on and their faces were black with the soot and smoke of the many fires. They ran to and fro, or bent over their work. One was blowing with a big bellows a fire that leaped up out of the rocky forge. Another was pushing a wheelbarrow full of gold ore, and still another one was standing guard over a heap of shining gems, that had been dumped in a corner.

They looked up as Annie came in. Every one touched his cap, and bowed low. Then there was a minute's stillness, and all at once they struck with their hammers on the anvils and sang the following song:

"Klink! klink! klinkety! klink!
Turn it and shape it as quick as a wink;
A beautiful cup, that a Princess may drink,
Rings for her fingers or bells for her feet,
All hammered out in the dust and the heat.

"Klink! klink! klinkety! kling!
A crown or a bracelet or any odd thing.
Next to Good Goldemar, Labor is King,
The harder we hammer, the louder we sing,
Klink! klink! klinkety! kling!

"Tink! tank! polish the heap,
The harder we labor the sweeter we sleep.
Every good workman is worthy his keep;
Worthy his keep and a diamond a day,
Shout all together, 'Hip, hip and hooray!'"

At the signal, "Shout all together," the workers lifted high their hammers and brought them down with such sounding blows upon the anvils, that Annie put her hands over her ears.

"It is a little loud for you as you are not accustomed to noises of bursting

rocks and roaring fires," said Grubel. "That was a salute they just now gave in your honor, and that song was made up by our Court Poet for you."

"I am sure it was very nice," said Annie, "only a little loud—it made my head ache. But why did they make a song for me?"

"Bless your heart, my little lady, that was in obedience to the King's command. You are to marry our young Prince Kuno to-morrow."

"I will not marry Prince Kuno!" cried Annie.

"Then, truly, dark days are in store for you," said old Grubel, sadly. "The King's will has never yet been crossed."

"Well, what will he do to me?" asked Annie.

"That, I can not tell," was the answer, "but something terrible, I fear."

The Old Gnome now led her to a little room, beautifully fitted up, which he told her was to be her own. The little girl lay down with her cat in her arms, and was soon sound asleep. The next morning she was awakened by a knocking on her door.

A Messenger had come to take her before the young Prince, who had returned from his hunting trip. Annie called Silvertip, and following the Messenger, they soon came to the Crystal Room, where the Prince was waiting to see them. He was a very handsome

Prince, not at all like the other Gnomes. His beautiful long curling hair fell down over his shoulders, and upon the jacket of his white velvet Court Suit. When he looked at her earnestly, Annie recalled the Prairie Dog, which she had saved from the steel trap, for there was the same peculiar expression in the eyes of the Gnome Prince.

He held out his wrist for Annie to see the scar upon it. "See," said he, "there are the marks yet of the teeth of that trap, from which you set me free last Midsummer Day. Do you remember, Annie?"

"I remember that I set a little Prairie Dog free from a steel trap a year ago, and I took him home.

But he ran away from me," said the little girl.

"Annie, it was I, myself, whom you saved that day, and I have never forgotten your kindness. Ask what you will of me, it shall be granted, on my honor as a Prince."

"Oh! then, if it please your Royal Highness, do just let me go back home to my own country. Give me my liberty, as I gave you your life," pleaded the child.

"The Prince looked very sad when he heard this. "Annie, think well," he said "before you leave us. Down here in our country you will be treated as though you were a Queen. A thousand Gnome Miners will drive their picks into the earth, seeking for gold and gems for you. You will live a beautiful life, and a long one. Will you not stay with me," he pleaded, "I have no one with whom to play, and I am so lonely sometimes."

"Your Royal Highness," replied the little girl, "I don't want to hurt your feelings, and I am sorry you are lonely. I know how it feels to be lonely myself, but though you do have the most rich and beautiful things down here that I ever saw in all my life, I would much rather go back to my own world, even with all the trouble there is in it. You are all so very different down here from the kind of folks I have lived with all my life, I am sure I should be just miserable. So, please, do help me to get away from your father, the Gnome King. He wants me to live down here and marry you, and he looks so stern and cross that I am afraid of him. Only show me the way out of here, and I will pray every night that God may send you a soul." Annie pleaded so earnestly to go home, that at last the young Prince felt sorry for her, and began to think how he could help her to get away from the Under World without letting his father know about it.

After thinking a little, the young Prince said: "There is just one thing for you to do in order to get away from here, and quite out of the power of my Father, the King. You must go out of

the castle by the secret passage and walk until you come to the big Wind Current, and step into it. It makes a dreadful roaring sound, and is very cold, but it will carry you up into the Sunshine all right. The Wind will land you in a wild spot high up among the hills. This spot, I think, is not far from the Enchanted Wood.

"Now listen carefully, while I tell you what to do when you get up to this place. You find your way to the good Witch Zauberlinda, ruler over all Pix-Sylvania. She spends Midsummer Week always at the Enchanted Wood, and all the birds and animals go up to meet her there at this time, for she lives all the rest of the year in her Palace at the end

of the Rainbow. She and the King are bitter enemies. Their lives and ways are utterly opposite each to the other. While he rules the Under World and all its glittering treasures of Gold and Gems, Zauberlinda is Queen of the Woods, Fields and Hills, of Flowers and Trees, Birds, Bees and all the Animals who roam through the forest. He is jealous of her power, but I, though a Gnome Prince, am not her enemy, for mixed with the Mist and Moonshine that runs in my veins, as it does in those of all the Gnomes, there is a drop of red human blood which has come down to me from a remote ancestor, on my Mother's side. This is why I am so different from all the others, and why I like you so much.

If you can find your way to Zauberlinda, she will send you safely home, for she is as good as she is wise, and she loves all young creatures."

Suddenly, while Annie stood in the Crystal Room talking with the young Prince, they heard some one calling out: "King Goldemar has lost his Signet Ring with the Magic Crystal. Who has stolen the Great Magic Crystal of the Gnomes?" Then there was great hurrying of the little Gnomes, to and fro, looking for the lost Signet Ring, and a great commotion reigned in King Goldemar's Castle.

Annie was dreadfully frightened. "I'm sure I have not stolen his Old Magic Crystal, why, I never stole any-

thing in all my life; but it would be just like these Gnome people to think I had stolen it, and I want to get away as soon as I can," she said, "for now the King will be in a dreadful rage."

"Come with me, then," cried the Prince, and Annie rushed after him, out of the Crystal Room, down a long passage way. She stopped beside a big flat stone, that seemed set into the floor. "Step upon that stone," said the Prince. "It will give way under your weight, and slowly sink down, until it lets you into the secret passage-way under the Castle; then you must walk straight ahead."

"Thank you, dear kind Prince," said Annie, "I shall never, never forget

you." She stepped upon the stone and called to him, "Goodbye." It sank down with her, until at last she stood in the secret passage way, Silvertip following her. She had not walked far when she heard the roar of the Wind Current, and a minute later the little girl was caught up by it and whirled along at a wonderful rate of speed. After she became accustomed to it, it was not so bad a way of traveling after all, anyhow, she was being whirled farther and farther away each moment from the dreadful Gnome King.

Chapter XII
Annie's Escape and the Fat-Heads

HER eyes to see what was ahead, Annie saw at last a faint glimmer of light. It grew brighter, she could smell new mown hay. At last, with a little whirl of the wind, she was thrown out upon a pile of newly cut green grass. Gasping to catch her breath, Annie looked up and saw the full round moon. The face in it had never before seemed to smile so kindly down upon her, as it did this night. She looked about, and saw that she was in a little Canyon, with high Mountains all around it. She could not see any houses, but right in front of her was a garden, with rows of cabbages and some lettuce beds. She walked over to look at the garden, and suddenly eame upon what looked like an army of big Fat-Heads, sticking up through the ground.

These heads had the ugliest faces any one could imagine; light streamed out of the big holes of eyes, and they had great grinning mouths with big teeth. Silvertip was rushing right toward them, but Annie caught him by the tail and pulled him back. Then she ran to the hay and sat down, hiding her eyes from them. A pretty white Rabbit was crouching in the hay right beside her, and it, too, was trembling with fear. "Poor Bunny, are you afraid of the dreadful Fat-Heads?" Bunny sat still and wriggled his nose, which was his way of answering "Yes."

The three of them crouched down in the shadow of the haycock. Annie hoped that the Fat-Heads would not see them. "I suppose we shall have to wait here until morning," said Annie to her Cat. "Don't you dare, sir, to touch the pretty Rabbit."

"Oh dear! Probably, we shall all be eaten up by those dreadful Fat-Heads, anyhow." Silvertip did not "Miaow"

in answer, she thought he must be sick, and tried to pry open his mouth to look at his tongue. He acted as though he had the lock-jaw, for he kept his teeth shut tightly together. But at last she managed to make the cat open his mouth. When this was done, something rolled out of it and on to the grass. Annie picked it up, and holding it in the moonlight, saw to her great surprise, that it was the Gnome King's Signet Ring.

Silvertip had picked it up and carried it away in his mouth, meaning to lay it finally in the lap of his little mistress. "Oh, Silvertip! You naughty Cat!" said Annie. "I am ashamed of you! How could you steal the King's Ring?"

At being scolded, Silvertip grew so wild and restless, that he gave one jump at the white Rabbit, and soon they were both off, helter skelter, over the cabbages and right in among the Fat-Heads. Annie thought it strange that the ugly faces never moved. "Well," thought the child, "If those things don't hurt my cat, it may be that they will not hurt me." So slowly and cautiously she walked straight up to them. Then she saw that the light was going out of their eyes. She knew then just what they were, and was so relieved of her fear, that she laughed and clapped her hands. "Why, they are nothing at all, but just some funny Jack O' Lanterns," she cried, and she was right.

Then Silvertip came back from the chase after the Rabbit. Annie took him in her arms, and they both lay down upon the new mown hay, to rest until morning.

It was broad day light when the little girl awoke from her sleep. Dew sparkled on the grass and flowers, everything smelled sweet, and looked cheerful and bright. Annie was happy, for she felt sure that if she could find her way to the Enchanted Wood, and see Zauberlinda, the Great Wise Witch would tell her the way to get home.

Silvertip had made his toilet early, and was out chasing butterflies. Annie smoothed her hair as well as she could, washed her hands and face in the dew,

and started out to find the inhabitants of this valley.

Wandering along, Annie finally came to a pretty pond, with water so clear she could see the little sun-fish darting through it waving their delicate fins. The banks that sloped toward the water were grassy, and she sat down and rested for a little while. Pretty soon some ducks came waddling down for their morning swim in the pond, and after them came some very white geese, with an old gray gander leading them. Behind them followed a queer looking, chubby little girl, driving the ducks and geese.

When the little goose-girl saw Annie, she stared a moment, her big eyes looking so surprised and frightened, that Annie laughed. Then she dropped her willow switch and ran as fast as her short legs would carry her, and as she ran she screamed with fright.

"Stop running so fast, I will not hurt you little girl," Annie called after her. The goose-girl would not turn around, but kept on running. "Well, thought Annie, so far I have not seen a house, nor met a man or woman in this valley, but there must be people living somewhere around, for there are gardens, and besides, that silly goose-girl must live somewhere, too."

Annie hurried down the canyon as fast as she could after the girl, and Silvertip after her. What was Annie's surprise to see the girl climb quickly up the side of a steep cliff that jutted out from the mountain walls of the canyon, and suddenly disappear.

"Dear me," said Annie to herself, "That is very much like the Gnomes' way of doing things, I do hope that the people who live in this canyon are not relations of the Gnomes, for I have had all I want of their company."

She began to feel very lonesome and home-sick, as well as exceedingly hungry and tired. She passed orchards, gardens and fields of corn, with geese and ducks in them, and pastures with cows and sheep feeding, but she never saw any houses or people.

At last, completely tired out, Annie

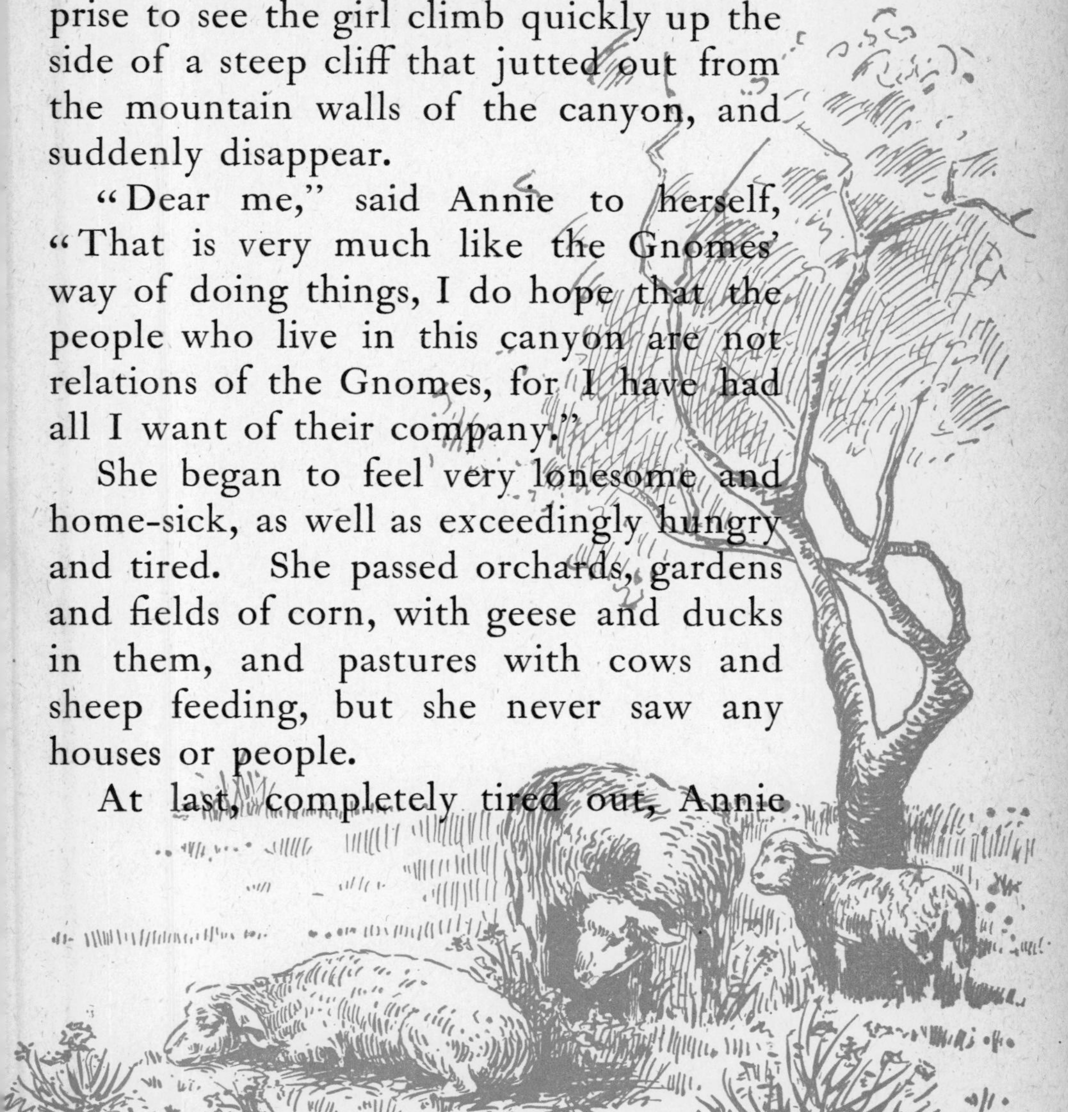

sat down on a boulder, to think what she should do. She was so hungry, that she felt she was nearly starving, but there was nothing to eat, except raw things. There were fine ears of green corn in the field, but she had no matches with which to light a fire to roast them.

As Annie sat thinking, with her head bent down and her eyes closed, she thought she smelled meat. Something fell into her lap, she looked, it was a duck, roasted and stuffed. Beside her sat Silvertip, licking his chops and blinking comically at her. Annie laughed aloud, and Silvertip, who had been watching her face, came up, and purred and rubbed his head against her knee.

"Naughty Silvertip!" said Annie, "first you stole the King's Signet Ring, and now you steal a roast duck, for you must have stolen it, nobody would ever give a roast duck to a strange cat."

"Miaow, miaow, miaow," said Silvertip.

"Yes, I understand, you mean to say that you stole it to bring it to me, because you love me so much. Of course, I shall have to forgive you this time, but if ever we get back home, you must change your ways and become a good honest cat, for it is very naughty to steal."

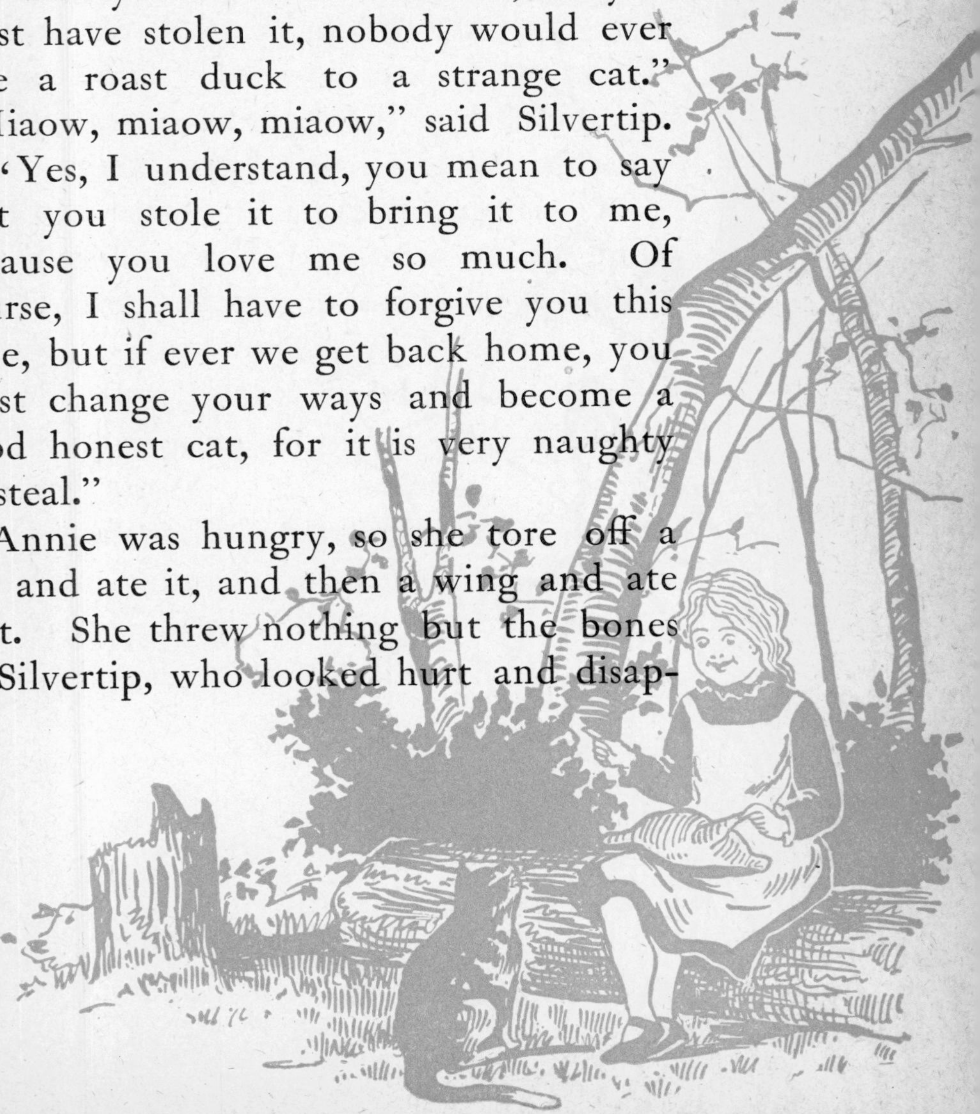

Annie was hungry, so she tore off a leg and ate it, and then a wing and ate that. She threw nothing but the bones to Silvertip, who looked hurt and disap-

pointed, but Annie knew that if she let him go without food until he was very hungry, the cat would be apt to sneak slyly back and try to find something more.

She meant to watch where he went, and follow him, for this seemed to be the only hope of finding the hidden homes of the strange people. As soon as the sun was over the mountain, it began to grow dark, though the moon was rising and lighted the valley softly with its silver beams.

Annie called Silvertip. They went back to the hay field and pulling the hay over them, to keep off the dew, she lay down beside the cat. She closed her eyes and breathed steadily, as though sleeping soundly. When the cunning cat thought his mistress asleep, he very cautiously got up, stretched himself and yawned. Then stepping softly, he soon began to trot along very swiftly through a wheat field. Annie followed him at a little distance. When he got out of the wheat, he went straight to the foot of the cliff, where the goose-girl had disappeared, and began to climb up the side.

Annie was so close now that she could see a flight of rough steps cut into the rock and leading up the side of the cliff. Annie followed the cat, climbing after him.

About half way up the cliff she stopped, for she saw that a little weather-beaten door had been put into the rocky wall in front of her. Not far from this was a little window, of just one pane of glass. Annie stood on the last and highest of the steps and knocked on the little rough door in front of her.

Chapter XIII
Annie Wanders Through the Valley of the Yubbs

NO ONE answered when Annie knocked at the door in the cliff; so, after waiting a little, she went back down the steps and wandered along through the valley, feeling very sad and lonely. She had not gone far when she met a little Indian boy, who smiled at her so pleasantly that she thought she would tell him her story, and ask him to show her the way out of this canyon.

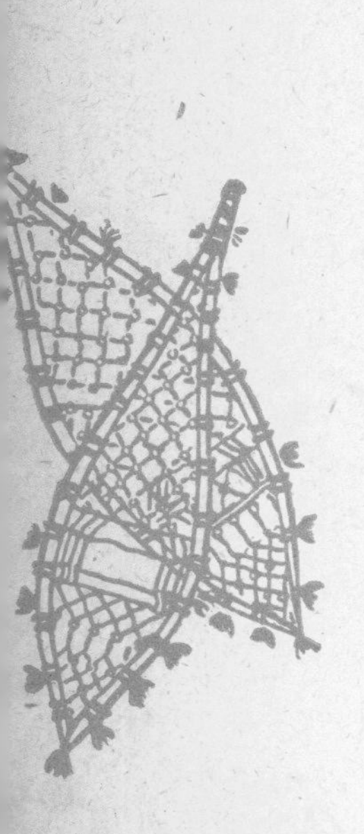

He told her that the valley was inhabited by a queer race of Cliff Dwellers, called Yubbs, who were so timid that they always ran and hid whenever a stranger appeared. The Indian boy said his name was Eagle Feather, and that he would guide her over the mountain to the Glade of the Enchanted Wood. He knew the place well, for it was there that his friends, the Wood-Folks in Fur and Feathers, assembled, from all the country around, in Midsummer Week, to hold a Council among themselves, away from their common enemy, Man, and to lay their grievances before their protector and friend, the Guardian Spirit of the Wild Woods, the Great Wise Witch Zauberlinda. He knew

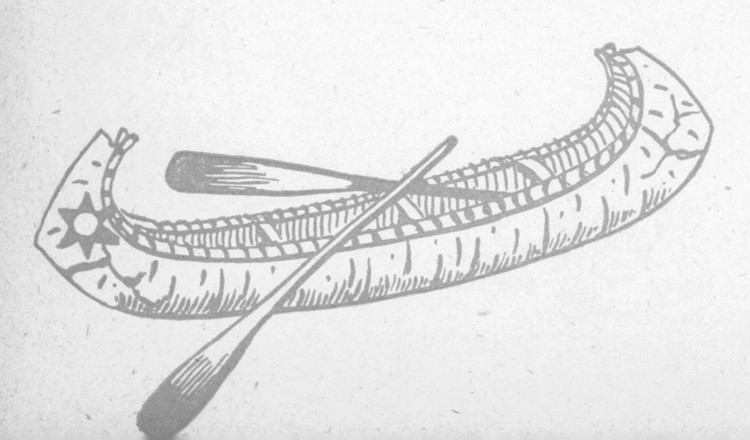

about her from the Big Medicine Man, who had trained him, and taught him how to talk with the birds and wild animals. Eagle Feather said he had started out to travel up to the Enchanted Wood himself to witness the Great Meeting. Annie was very glad that he would take her along as she liked and trusted him the minute she saw him.

Eagle Feather was a handsome boy, with his clear, dark skin and black laughing eyes; when he smiled at Annie showing his white teeth, his face was very winning and pleasant. He was beautifully dressed, as was fitting for the son of a Great Chief. He wore a buckskin jacket, which was fringed all the way down the front and all around

the bottom and the sleeves. His moccasins were handsomely embroidered with bright red, yellow and green hedge-hog quills. Upon the breast of his jacket queer devices and strange fantastic figures were worked in gay colored beads. Around his forehead and head, and holding back his long, glossy, black hair, was fastened an embroidered leather band, from the back of which, and pointing to the front, over his head, projected a large gray eagle's feather. Slung over his left shoulder, and fastened together under his right arm, he carried his bright colored blanket. As the son of a Great Chief, and also as the adopted son of the Medicine Man of Red Cloud's tribe,

he carried himself proudly, and with a certain child-like dignity.

Eagle Feather thought it would be best to start out at once, he said, as the Enchanted Wood lay far away. So leaving behind them the Canyon of the timid Yubbs, the little Pale-Face and the Indian boy started out to travel over the mountains.

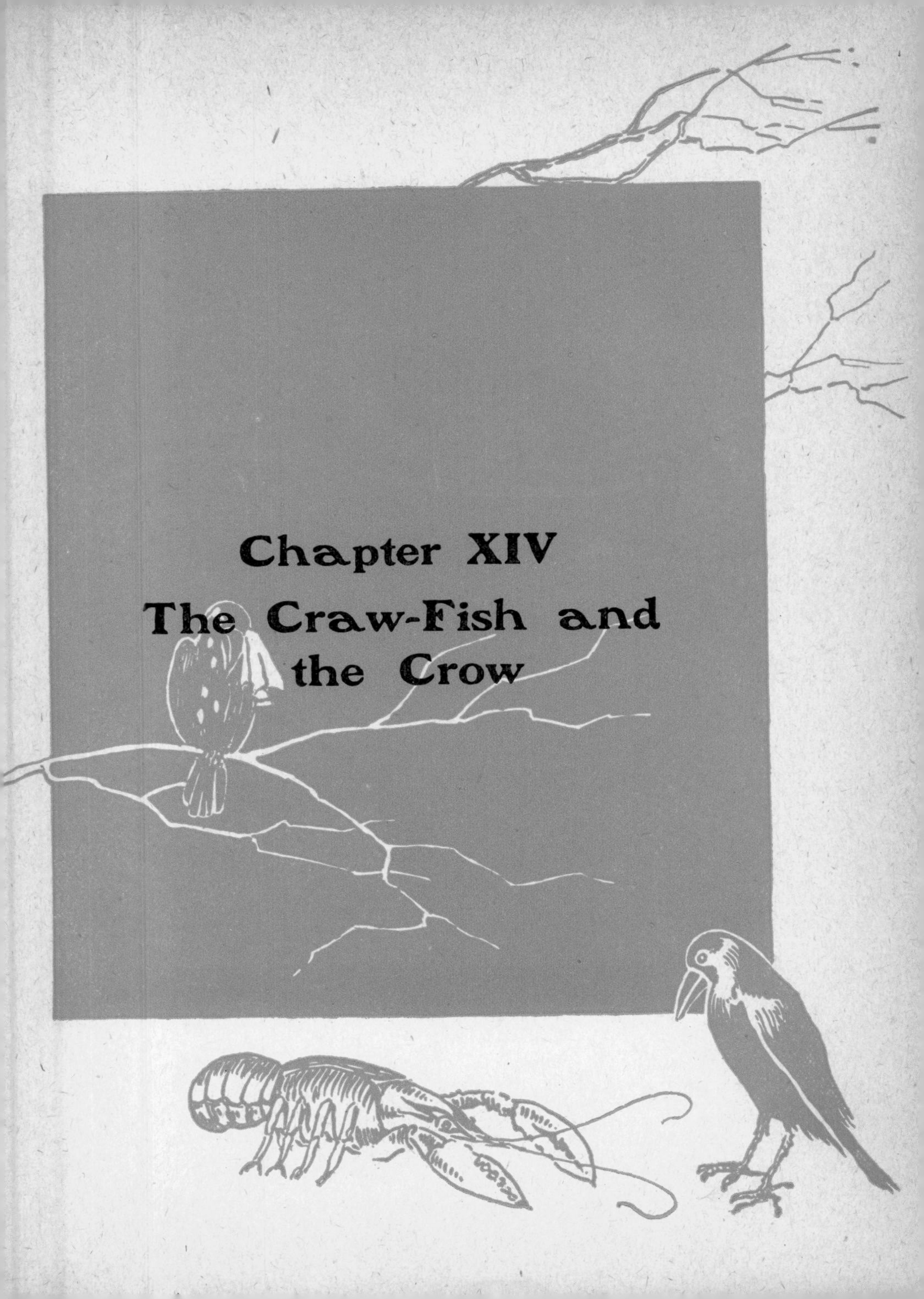

Chapter XIV
The Craw-Fish and the Crow

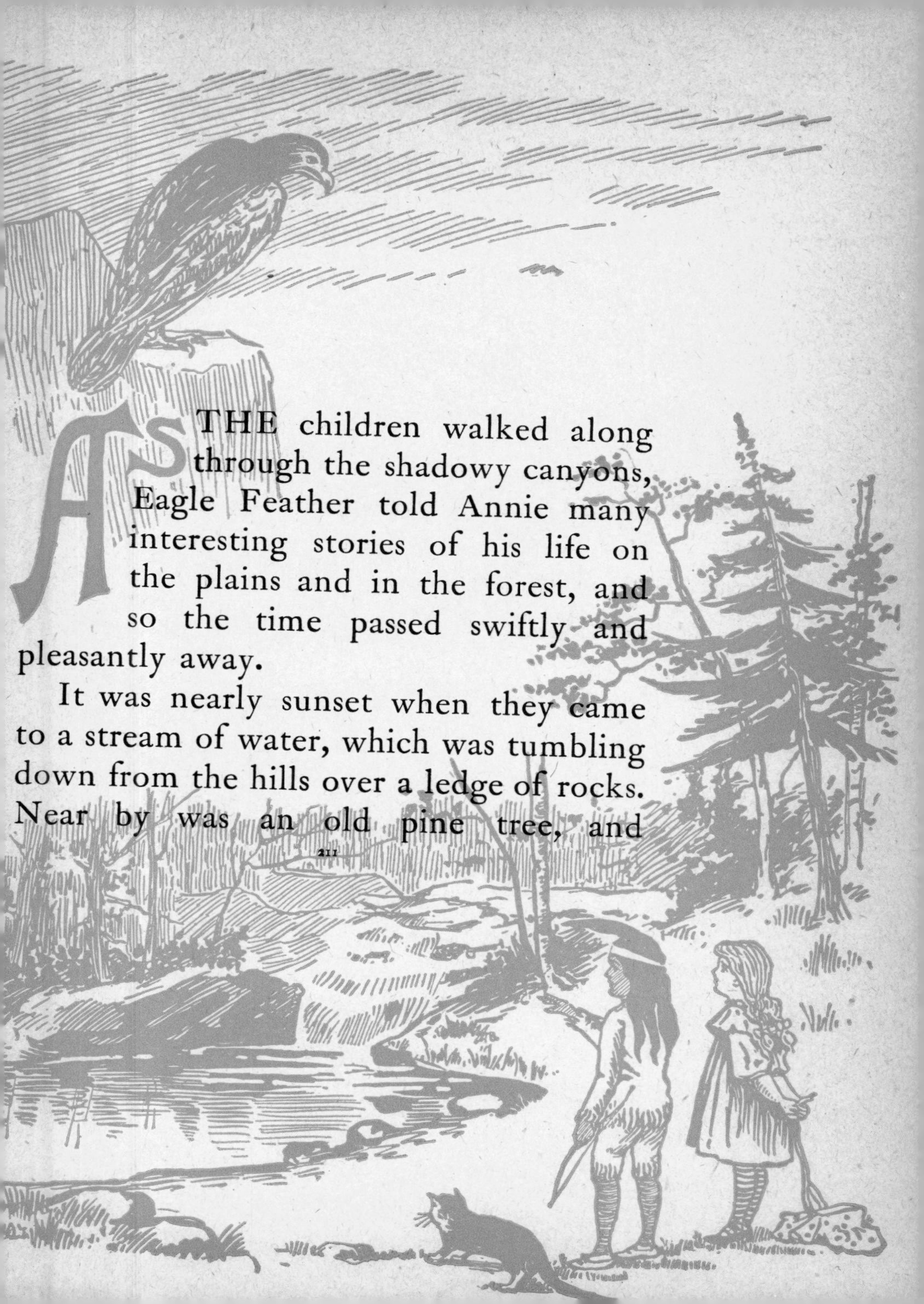

AS THE children walked along through the shadowy canyons, Eagle Feather told Annie many interesting stories of his life on the plains and in the forest, and so the time passed swiftly and pleasantly away.

It was nearly sunset when they came to a stream of water, which was tumbling down from the hills over a ledge of rocks. Near by was an old pine tree, and

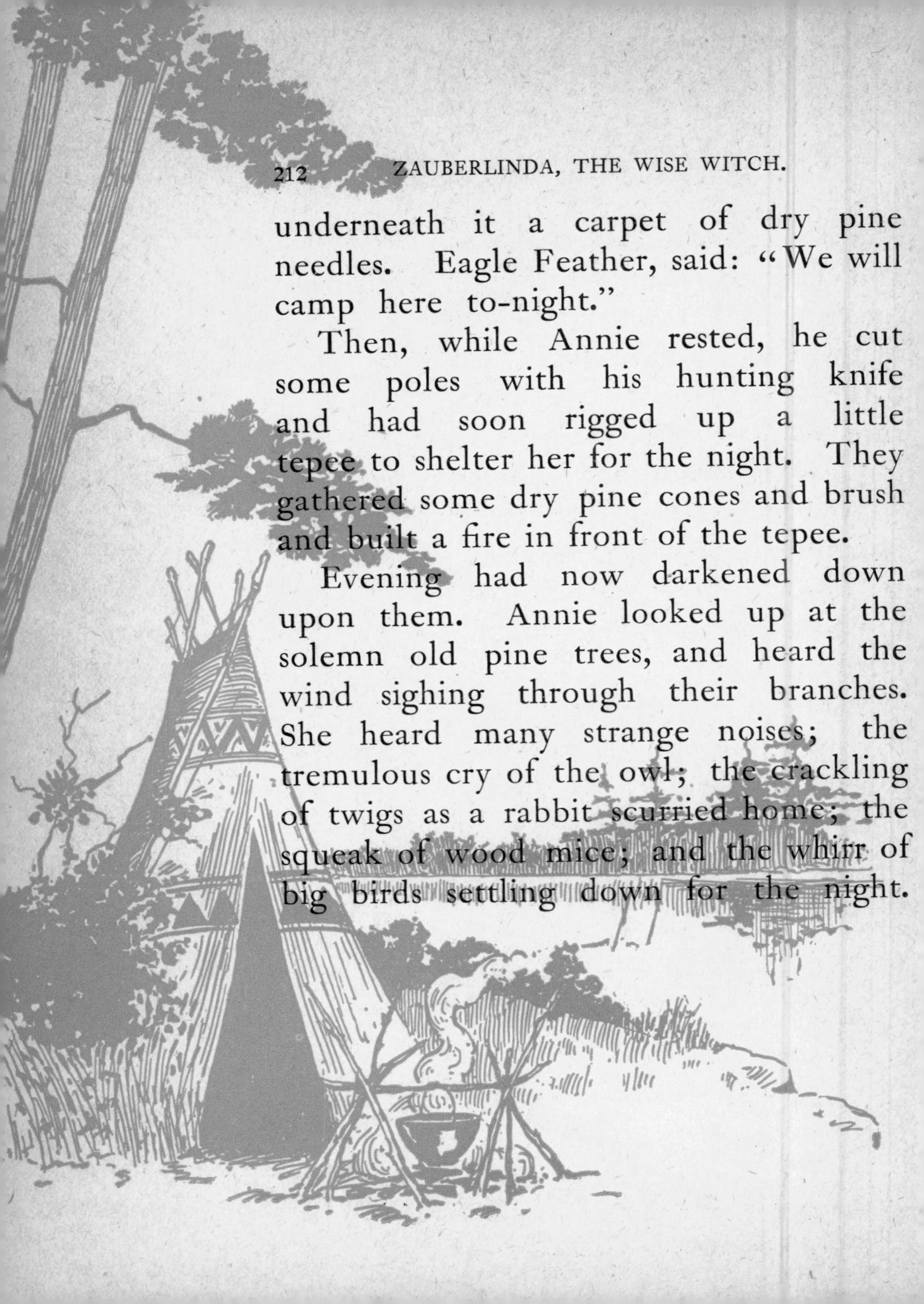

underneath it a carpet of dry pine needles. Eagle Feather, said: "We will camp here to-night."

Then, while Annie rested, he cut some poles with his hunting knife and had soon rigged up a little tepee to shelter her for the night. They gathered some dry pine cones and brush and built a fire in front of the tepee.

Evening had now darkened down upon them. Annie looked up at the solemn old pine trees, and heard the wind sighing through their branches. She heard many strange noises; the tremulous cry of the owl; the crackling of twigs as a rabbit scurried home; the squeak of wood mice; and the whirr of big birds settling down for the night.

She looked out into the dark shadows and fancied she could see queer faces looking at her from the gnarled trunks of the old trees. Once or twice a will-o-the-wisp flitted by, and Annie was sure she saw a Wood Sprite's face peering at her from the branches overhead.

As they wanted to rise early in the morning, Eagle Feather made Annie go to rest. Then he wrapped himself in his blanket and lay down beside the camp fire.

As they lay resting the birds began to sing softly in the trees overhead. "They are talking to the Great Spirit," said Eagle Feather. "Everything in the forest speaks to Him at night, thanking Him for another day of sunshine and life. Everything in the woods awakens when the East is red, and talks again to the Great Spirit. Then the birds sing their song of praise to Him; the flowers lift up their little cups, all filled with dew, and pour out their fragrance upon the air. That is their praise to the Great Spirit, who lives over the stars."

Soon the little white girl and the dark skinned Indian boy were sound asleep in the heart of the Ancient Woods; and while they slept, all around them was the tread of padded feet walking over the pine needles, the flutter of wings, the calling of moose, the howl of wolves, the cry of mountain lions, the grunt of a bear as he shambled along in the darkness, for all the Wood-Folks were on their way to the place of the Great Meeting. Occasionally a big dusky form would come to the camp fire and pause a moment, looking at the little sleepers, and then pass on. Overhead great flocks of geese, ducks and sand hill cranes were flying and calling to each other shrilly, all hurrying on to the Meeting Place.

Once Eagle Feather awakened in the night, and hearing the commotion all around and overhead, smiled, then turning over, and wrapping his blanket more closely around him, he said, softly: "My brothers in Fur and Feathers are traveling far to-night; there will be a great company to welcome Zauberlinda to-morrow."

The next morning Eagle Feather arose before the sun was up, and caught some trout in the mountain stream. These he rolled up in leaves and clay, and baked in hot ashes. By the time Annie was up, Eagle Feather had the breakfast cooked, and they washed their hands and faces in the mountain stream, and sat down to eat. While they were at breakfast, various travelers came along and joined their company. Eagle Feather interpreted to Annie the strange sounds they made in talking in their own odd way.

Among the birds who began to arrive was a dignified Black Crow, who came

hopping along, cocking his head to one side, his shining round black eyes full of prying curiosity.

The company was proving so interesting that Eagle Feather and Annie concluded to make a day of it and rest there in the shade. A Pigeon and a Sand Hill Crane joined their company. An old, rheumatic, sarcastic looking green Parrot,—who had run away from a Young Ladies' Seminary,—waddled up to them on her crooked legs, and Ki-Yi, a very retiring Coyote, sidled cautiously up and took a seat on the edge of the queer circle before the Tepee.

Annie thought sometimes that she surely must be dreaming, it was so strange to see such a company assembled.

There were Bears, Rabbits and Squirrels, Coyotes and Mountain Lions and Rocky Mountain Sheep, Beavers, Muskrats, Mink and many other animals, all apparently on friendly terms.

There were song birds of every variety and color and from every clime, and birds of bright plumage. There were assembled Robins, Orioles, Mocking-birds, Thrushes and Meadow-larks. Finally a Meadow-lark suggested a song. After much coaxing a Thrush sang a Ballad that was so sweet and full of tenderness, there was not a dry eye in the whole assembly.

After the Thrush's sweet song, the hush that followed was broken by a long, low, heart-broken wail. It came from

Ki-Yi, who remarked that he was sad to-day, as he was grieving over the loss of his brother. Said poor Ki-Yi: "We both started out yesterday together, to come up to the Great Meeting; but the villainous Cowboys caught sight of us, gave chase, and shot and killed my brother. He was my only friend, and now that he is dead, I don't want to live any longer."

To give the conversation a more cheerful turn, a clever Mocking Bird from the South gave an imitation of every bird in the forest. He mimicked them so well that it made every one laugh. Finally the green Parrot offered to sing a ballad, which she said she had learned from the old Yankee Sailor who had brought her up and trained her in the art of public speaking, before she lived with the mistress of the Young Ladies' School.

No one urged Poll to sing. She paid no attention to their silence, however, but hopped up on the limb of a tree, and clinging to it with her ugly hooked claws balanced herself, struck an attitude, and sang in a husky voice the following ballad:

Once in a pretty woodland,
Near a cabin 'way out West,
In a lightnin'-blasted Tam'rack Tree,
An Old Crow built his nest;
And there did he his family,
In the way that they should go,—
Raise up, and all were dutiful
But the oldest son, Jim Crow.

CHORUS

Caw,-Caw,-Caw,
'Tis the saddest tale I know,
This tragic story I relate
Of the Crawfish and the Crow.

Young Jim Crow he was venturesome,
Much praise his head had swelled,
And so against all good advice
His young Crow-pride rebelled.
"If I may not look into *life*,
Whatever shall I know?
The thing for me is novelty,"
Says reckless young Jim Crow.

One day a curious kind of fish
Young James Crow he espied,
A-sunnin' on a sandy bank,
A runnin' stream beside;
And why it wore its bones outside,
And had such nipper claws,
Jim, maybe 'cause he was a Crow,
Desired to learn the cause.

Says Father Crow: "Take warnin', Jim,
And don't ye peek and peer,
Ner poke yer pryin' little bill
Inter everything that's queer;

But Jim, a-peckin' at its feet,
For novelty did seek;
He found it, for that queer Craw-Fish
Just caught him by the beak.

Jim couldn't caw, he couldn't call,
He couldn't croak ner cry;
The Craw-Fish clutchin' onto him,
All 'round and 'round he'd fly.
And so with it a hangin' on
And clingin' to his bill,
The skeleton of poor Jim Crow
Just keeps on flyin' still.

MORAL.

Now, all you little birds, beware
The fate of young Jim Crow,
Leave other folks's things alone,
And let strange fishes go;
And don't ye touch, and don't ye taste,
And don't ye pry and peer,
And keep your little bills away
From things unknown and queer,
And mind your eyes and dodge the guns,
And take advice from me:
Avoid Jim Crow's besettin' sin
Of Cu-ri-os-i-tee.

Chapter XV
Annie Meets Zauberlinda

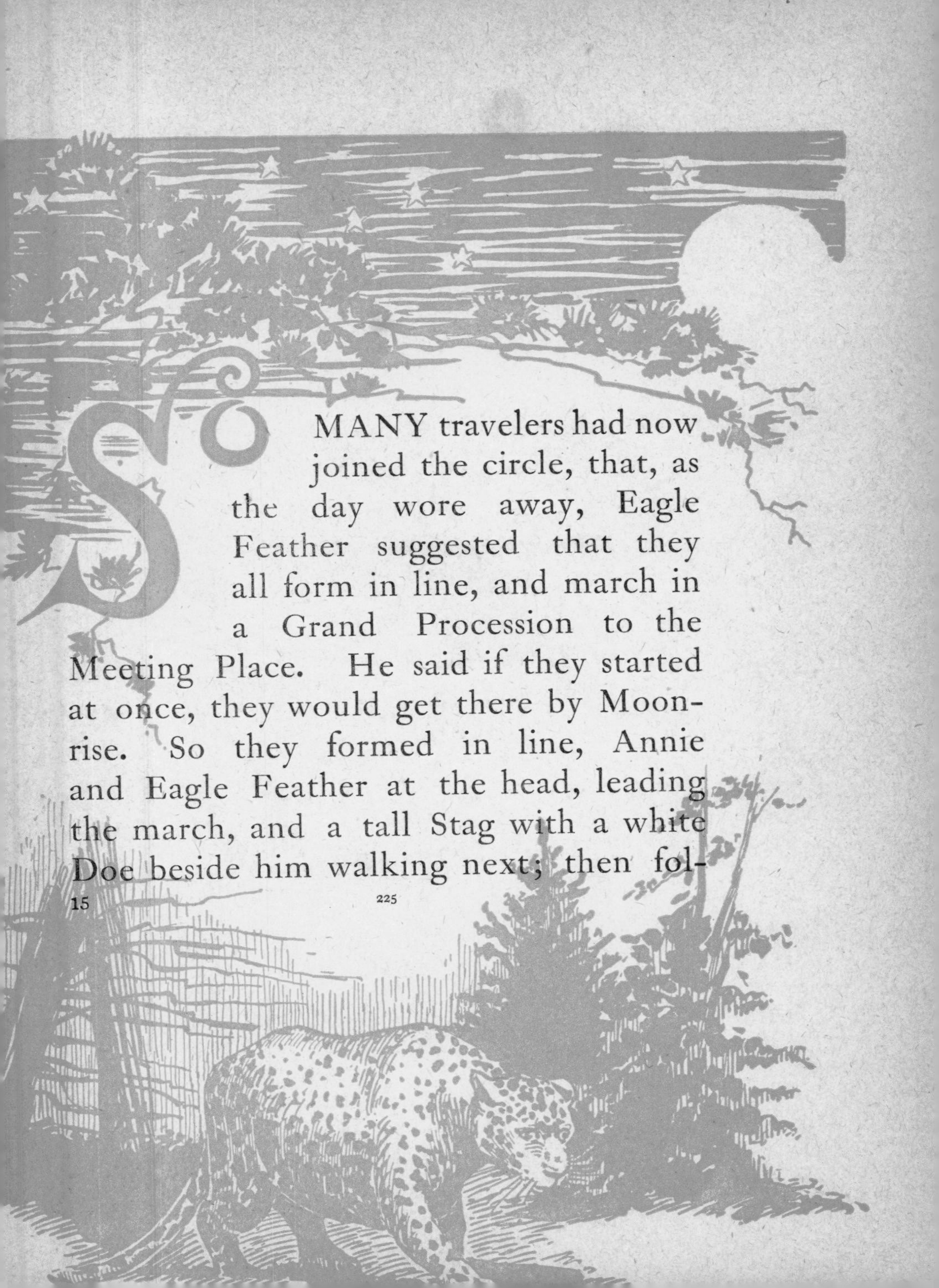

SO MANY travelers had now joined the circle, that, as the day wore away, Eagle Feather suggested that they all form in line, and march in a Grand Procession to the Meeting Place. He said if they started at once, they would get there by Moon-rise. So they formed in line, Annie and Eagle Feather at the head, leading the march, and a tall Stag with a white Doe beside him walking next; then followed two Antelopes; after them came some Rocky Mountain Sheep, while two very jolly Bears walked side by side and amused the company with their drolleries. The long Procession was followed by numerous bands of small creatures. Prince Limberlegs, a big Bull-Frog, led the army of Green Jumpers. Over-head, great flocks of Wild Ducks and Geese and Cranes, were calling and clamoring. All was hub-bub and confusion. They were all humming, buzzing, quacking, grunting, barking, yelping, singing or calling to each other, as they marched along through the forest. The Meeting Place was in the heart of the Enchanted Wood near a clear pretty lake, where the out-

stretched arms of great trees made a deep shade.

Fireflies had flung themselves in chains of light, over the tall reeds by the lake, to illuminate the place, and white Night-Moths fluttered like flags from the branches and twigs of the old trees. It was a wonderful, dazzling, and beautiful sight. Hundreds of Animals were already there when the Procession arrived. Some birds of very beautiful plumage, had come to beg Zauberlinda to change their pretty feathers to duller, more ugly colors, because the rare beauty of their plumage often brought down upon them a cruel death, as they were hunted for their breasts and wings. They feared they would all be exterminated if something was not done for them very soon. "Yes," said the Buffalo, "it will be with them, as it was with us. Once we roamed the plains in herds that numbered thousands, now, alas! there are but few of us left."

When Eagle Feather interpreted this to Annie, she pitied the Buffalo, and the pretty birds so much, that her eyes were filled with tears for their sad fate, and she declared that she would never again wear the breast or wing of a bird on her hat. The company was very noisy at first, but when a big white Owl called "To-wit! To-woo!' a hush fell over everything. Annie looked down a forest aisle, where the moonlight fell like a river of light, and dashing down through it, with their proud heads high in the air, came two splendid milk-white Moose at full speed. Their branching horns were garlanded with woodland ferns and flowers, and their great soft black eyes gleamed in the moonlight. They drew a beautiful Chariot covered with wood-lichen and toadstools, pink, yellow, drab and streaky green ones. Upon a throne-like seat in this Chariot, sat a beautiful Being with white arms and gleaming shoulders. Her face was radiant, smiling and young. Her flowing mantle was all of forest green. A wreath of wild wood-land flowers and rushes was on her lovely head, with its long silky flowing hair. A light seemed to shine all around her but one could not see from whence it came. Two big white Rabbits sat up behind her Chariot and a white Owl was perched upon her shoulder. She carried a long wand with a gleaming "Z" on the end of it. Her two white Moose drew up with a flourish in the center of the open space near the lake in full view of all the eager watchful eyes.

There was a moment of silence. Then the Night Birds struck up a loud chorus—whip-poor-wills, owls and thrushes seemed to vie with the droning gnats, the tree-toads and the bullfrogs, with their deep bass voices. Zauberlinda raised her Magic Wand—all was hushed. Then at a signal three brown bears shambled out from the assembly

and began to climb up into a tree as quickly and as quietly as possible. Then some more bears came out into the open space and danced, opening their great mouths and showing their white teeth. Finally they played some games and ended by all joining hands and dancing around the tree, like children playing "Ring-around-a-Rosy."

Suddenly they scattered and ran. When the owl called "To-Woo," they squatted so quickly and became so motionless that one could not tell them from old brown tree stumps, which is just what the bears wanted, for it is one of their ways of hiding from their enemies.

After the Bear plays, the Wolves gave an exhibition of their skill, and the

Coyotes showed off their accomplishments.

Annie who had always loved and defended the Wild Animals, sat very still, her big blue eyes shining with excitement and interest. She said that one of the prettiest things she saw at the Midsummer Meeting, was the dance of the Sand Hill Cranes. First they stood up in line like awkward long legged soldiers, just learning to drill. They courtesied, then danced on one foot, then upon the other and zigzagged back and forth to their first places again.

After the animals had performed, they filed past Zauberlinda, who spoke to one a word, touched another lightly with her Wand, or reproved still another, which

hung its head and slunk away ashamed. Annie watched everything wonderingly. Suddenly, her heart throbbed faster. As though by some command which they could not disobey, Annie and Eagle Feather arose at the same time, and hand in hand through the throng of wild animals they walked up to the chariot of the Great Wise Witch. She looked into their faces and smiled, and her smile was like the sun when it lights the forest aisles on a May morning, and all the little new leaves tremble for joy.

"Speak! my children. What brings you to my Forest Glade?" she said.

"Oh, Wise Zauberlinda," answered Eagle Feather, bending low before her, "I have come that I might ask you to put it into the hearts of my Pale-Face Brothers to spare to us children of Nature still a few wild places, like this wood of yours, so that my own people, and my friends, the Wood Folks, may not all perish from the earth."

"Thou hast spoken well," said Zauberlinda. "Mother Nature shall know thy wish. She will open the blind, unseeing eyes of men to the wild beauty of Her still and shadowy places, and inspire their hearts with a truer worship and love of Her, and with kindness and pity for Her wild children."

Eagle Feather turned away.

It was now Annie's turn to speak. She took from her little pocket the Gnome King's Ring, set with the Magic

Crystal. She held it up in the moonlight, and told the Wise Witch, honestly and bravely, how it had come into her possession. "Let me look at it more closely," said the Wise Witch. Annie waited while Zauberlinda gazed earnestly into the great gleaming Crystal.

"Dost grant me permission to do with this as I will?" she asked Annie. The child bowed her head. "Then," said Zauberlinda, lifting it with a sweep of her white arm, high above her head, "Thus do I hurl the thing far from thee, and with it the curse which forever follows the use of Unearned Gold. Come, Nix, old Water Nix, come and take this bauble and give it to thy mermaids to play with, or if thou wilt use it to find

gold, keep what thou dost gain to gild the scales of thy gold and silver fish."

Annie was so surprised at this unexpected way of dealing with the Magic Crystal, that she could not speak, yet suddenly she began to feel very glad, light hearted and gay. All her troubles seemed to have slipped away from her, as the ring sank down to the bottom of the lake.

"Child Annie, come closer," said Zauberlinda, still with a sweet smile upon her face. "Thou art not vexed that I flung away that evil thing?"

"No, for whatever the good Wise Witch does, must surely be right," said the child softly.

"Never more wilt thou have cause to

fear the Gnome King," said Zauberlinda, "For, when this ring sank to the bottom of the lake, he lost forever all power over thee. What dost thou wish of me now?"

"Above all things, to go home to my own people," said Annie, "to grandmother, my papa, and dear Pete Pumpernickel."

"I will have thee taken home by the straightest, shortest way, by my own white-winged sky-ships," said Zauberlinda. "But first, since I have taken away the Gold-Finding Crystal, I will give thee something in its place, for I have ever loved thee, for thy sweet pity for my wild creatures of Wood and Plain and Field. Listen, child Annie,

I touch thee with my Magic "Z" and the charm shall abide with thee forever. Upon thine eyes, with my magic wand I touch thee and bestow upon thee the gift of the Seeing Eyes. Thou shalt see and know the beauty of God's wild woodland things, the soft eye of the Deer, the sheen upon the Dragon Fly's wing and the grace and beauty of the White Heron.

"Upon thy breast I touch thee and bestow upon thee, the gift of the Feeling Heart. Thou shalt have sympathy for all living things. Upon the lips I touch thee and bestow upon thee the gift of Eloquent Speech, Thou shalt speak ever the right words for all my dumb creatures, who suffer in silence and are abused and misunderstood. Rise, Child Annie, little Sister of Pity and Princess of the Enchanted Wood, Go out and teach the great lesson of kindness."

Annie arose, her heart swelling as if it would break with pride and happiness.

"Great and Good Zauberlinda," she said, "I thank you with all my heart and I will always try to faithfully obey your wishes, and I shall come back every year to sit at your feet at the Great Meeting, with my friends in Fur and Feathers, and with them learn the lessons you teach."

But now, streaks of crimson light began to shoot up in the eastern sky and a flute-like note from a watching bird, broke the silence that had fallen over all the Woods.

"I must away," said the Great Wise Witch. "Midsummer Week is over and past." She waved her Magic Wand and in an instant the beasts and birds had scattered and disappeared in the shadowy forest. Eagle Feather, too, had vanished. Zauberlinda lifted her lovely face and turned it Eastward to the rising sun, then holding up her white arms to the blue sky she called:

"Over water, over land,
From beyond the Golden Strand,
Come, white ships that sail the sky,
Hither, hither, hither fly."

Instantly three great white gulls came flying from the east and alighted at

Annie's feet. They carried a basket woven from stout green rushes.

Annie heard the voice of Zauberlinda saying, "I must away to my palace at the end of the shining rainbow." The child looked around just in time to see Zauberlinda in the chariot and the White Moose going at full speed down the Woodland Aisle. She turned and stepped into the basket-boat. The gulls began to rise in the air, she closed her eyes and could feel that their strong wings were bearing her up. She thought to see Harney's Peak from away up in the sky, and so opening her eyes to look down for a minute she found herself instead looking——right into her father's face, for she was being lifted up in his strong arms.

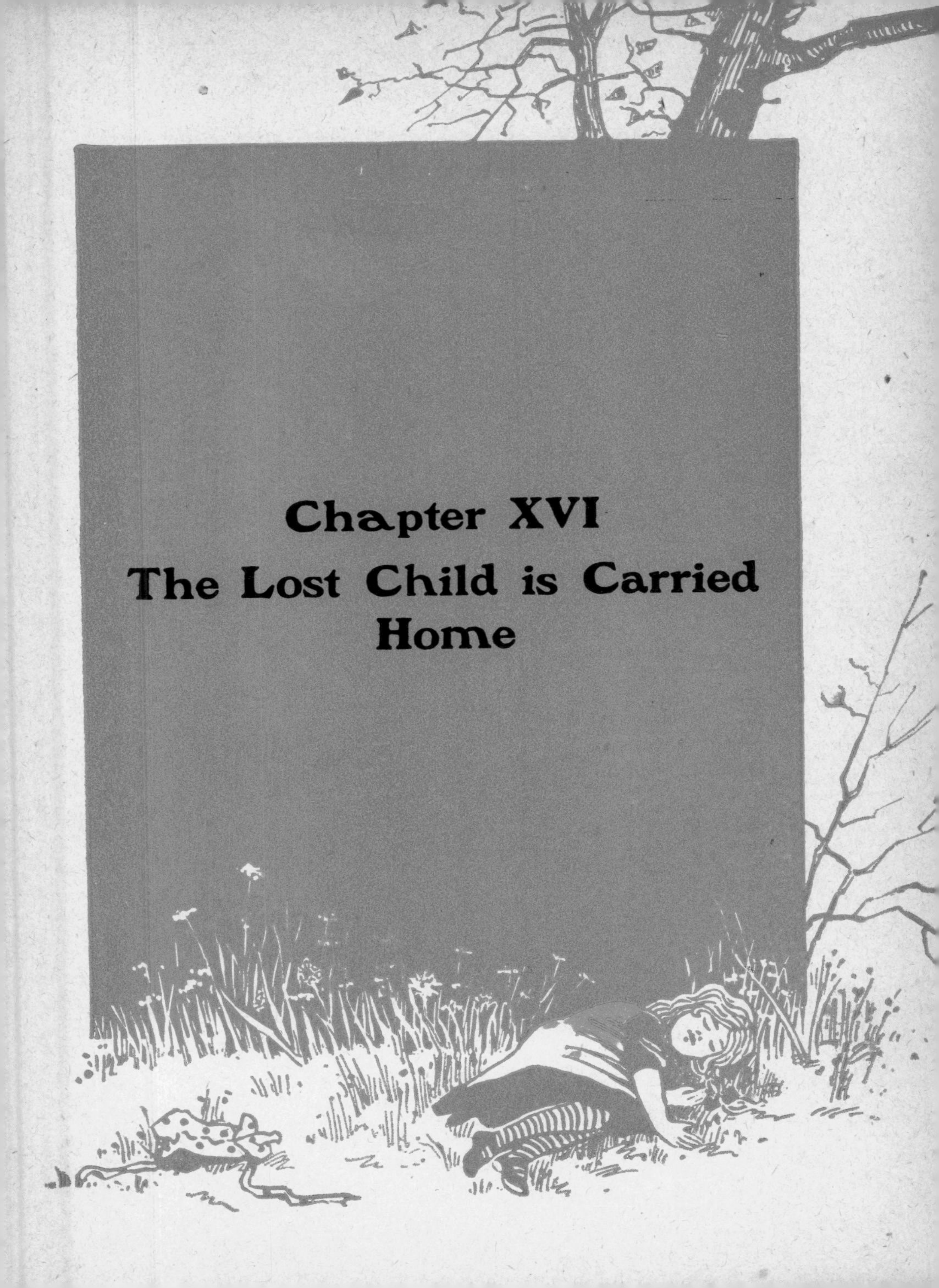

Chapter XVI
The Lost Child is Carried Home

Annie LEANED her head back against her father's strong shoulder and looked wonderingly around her. It was dusk. Silvertip was purring, rubbing his head against her father's legs, and trying to get up to Annie's face to welcome her.

"Where are the nice big gulls?" said Annie.

"They must be flying overhead," said

her father. "Thank God, you are here instead of at the bottom of the creek." Then he hugged the child and kissed her a great many times. She saw that her father carried a lantern, and very soon Pete Pumpernickel came up, and Annie was surprised to see that Professor Pratt was with him, and they, too, carried lanterns. They said, "Thank Heaven," and seemed to be very glad to have found her. Annie was still thinking of Zauberlinda and could not understand why everybody was so glad.

They carried her home. Her grandmother met them at the door and clasped Annie close in her arms. Grandmother's eyes looked red, as though she had been crying.

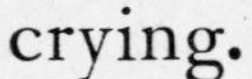

Then a pretty lady, whose dress had a sweet smell like violets, took Annie in her arms, and she, too, kissed her and cried. They told her that this lady was Aunt Molly, who had arrived there from Chicago that day. Annie liked her, she had such a pretty face; something like Zauberlinda's, Annie thought. Then a timid little girl with long yellow curls and a pale sweet face was led up and introduced to Annie as Lizzie May. She had brought Annie a beautifully dressed doll from Chicago, which could open and shut its eyes, and when you squeezed its stomach in the right place it would say "Ma-Ma" in a squeaky voice.

Annie, who had always thought to herself that she certainly should hate

Lizzie May, if ever she met her, was now happily surprised to find herself liking her.

Every one was very kind to Annie. The child could not understand what the fuss was all about, until Marthy Stubbs told her that she had been lost all day. They had missed her until the livery had brought her Papa, and Professor Pratt, and her aunt Molly over from Cave City. Then they all asked for Annie; it was found she had not been seen since morning. When six o'clock came, and the little girl had not come home, they all began to grow alarmed and anxious. They started out to search for her, and Pete had discovered her old doll stranded on a mud bank nearly a

mile down the creek. This had frightened them terribly, for they thought Annie must have fallen into the creek and drowned. Marthy's voice trembled as she told this to Annie, and then she too caught Annie up and kissed and hugged her.

The child had never been made so much of before, in all her life. They had a nice supper that evening, and, although it was late, Grandmother made one of her famous Strawberry Shortcakes with some berries Pete had brought from Cave City. Everybody seemed to love Annie very much, and when at supper, she and Lizzie May, sat one on each side of her Father, there was not a happier, prouder little girl

in all South Dakota than Annie Elfrida McLane.

After supper, Pete was requested to bring down his zither and play as they were all in such an excited state of mind, and Grandmother said that music always soothed her nerves. Pete played some old German airs and then his favorite tune entitled, "Sweet Dreamland Faces."

Annie told them, as well as she could, her experience with the Gnomes and Zauberlinda. They listened, smiling mysteriously and winking too, sometimes, at each other as though they thought she really did not know what she was talking about. When she had related the tale of her adventures in Pix-Sylvania—perhaps not exactly as it is written here,

although the writer has endeavored to tell it much in the same way that Annie told it to her friends—everybody had something to say.

Annie's father took her on his knee, stroking back her hair from her forehead, with his rough, kind hand in the old way, as he said: "Well, little daughter, your old Pap has struck 'pay dirt' at last and struck it rich too. Now, we'll all go to Chicago, Annie, and you shall be sent to school. Now I'll get a piano for you. But you ought to have brought me that Magic Crystal, I could have made such good use of it, I guess Pete and I had better fish for it in the creek." "It was a big Lake Zauberlinda threw the ring into," said Annie, quite seriously.

"The old water Nix will never let you have it, he wants to use it to find gold and silver to gild the scales of his gold and Silver Fish with."

Then Professor Pratt took Annie and holding her between his knees, felt of the bumps of her head. Said the Professor, "Great Ideality here, sir, vivid Imagination. In educating this child, I would advise a study of the Exact Sciences, let us say Mathematics, nothing like them to develop the reasoning faculties."

The best part of her home-coming to the little girl was that evening, over in the corner of the kitchen, when Marthy was washing her supper dishes, and Pete Pumpernickel was smoking a long-stemmed pipe, with a china bowl, and

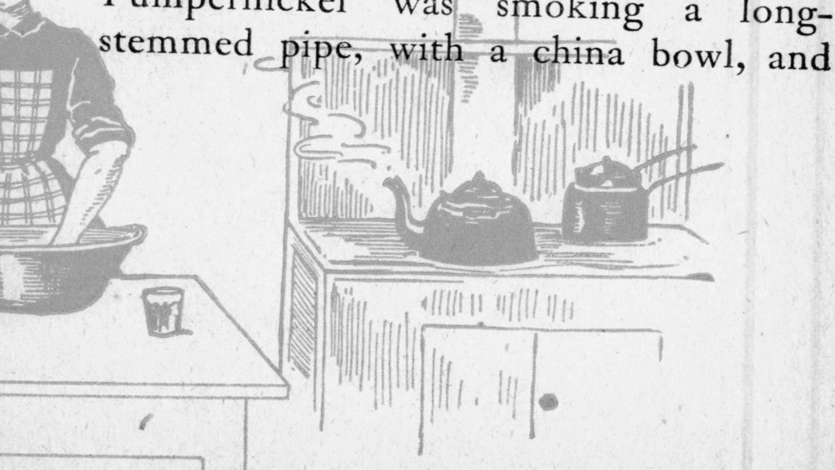

a picture of the old Goslar Kaiser-House on it. "Come to me, my Annie," whispered Pete, "I have a little gift for your birthday. I sent clear over to Germany for it, to my uncle, who keeps a book store near Leipzig. It is a book which is called 'Fairy Tales.' It is printed in German, but Pete will put it in English for you."

Annie took the book, which was full of beautiful pictures, and thanked Pete earnestly. It seemed that after all Pete had not forgotten that she was just seven years old upon that midsummer day.

"There now! You want to fill that child's head with some more crazy German stuff about the Gnomes and Goblins, and all such," said Marthy.

"Here she has been out on the prairie all this afternoon dreaming of them and pretty near got a sunstroke from it."

"Oh, no, Marthy, I have been in such a beautiful place, with the Good Witch Zauberlinda," said Annie.

"You've been asleep on the hot prairie, down by the creek," said Marthy, "and so, poor lamb, you don't know what you are talking about at all."

Annie looked over to Pete appealingly, and as usual he understood her better than anybody else. She was so glad that she had refused to wed the Gnome Prince and had remained faithful to Pete. The simple, kind fellow put his arm around the child tenderly, drawing her closely to his side. Slowly and calmly he took the long pipe from his lips; then looking dreamily into the child's trustful eyes, which were as clear and blue as the beautiful Dakota sky, he said, "My Annie has been away with the Fairy People."

* * * * * * * *

And thus our little western girl, whose life had been one of such monotony as only a child on a western prairie farm knows, came to learn in her dream of the wonders of Fairy Land and the Under World. While much is fancy, still there is more in the realm of Nature than is dreamed of in our philosophy.

"Golden notes of welcome rolled
Never forth such notes, nor told
Hours so blithe, in tones so bold
As the radiant mouth of gold
Here, that rings forth heaven.
If the golden crested wren
Were a nightingale—why, tnen,
Something seen and heard of men
Might be half as sweet as when
Laughs a child of seven."